MO...

Welcome to Big Sky Country, home of the Montana Mavericks! Where free-spirited men and women discover love on the range.

THE TENACITY SOCIAL CLUB

In rough-and-tumble Tenacity, it seems everyone already knows everyone else—*and* their business. Finding someone new to date can be a struggle. But what if your perfect match is already written in the stars? Pull up a barstool and open your heart, because you never know who you might meet at the Social Club!

Nina Sanchez did her best to leave Barrett Deroy in the past. Her first and only love left town without a word fifteen years ago, and she never heard from him again. Now that Barrett is back, they can't just pick things up where they left off. She's not the same person she once was; the boy she loved is gone. And yet Nina can't help longing to be in Barrett's arms one more time...

Dear Reader,

There's something special about a cousin. I have a big, extended family. Aunts, uncles, cousins—I even have some cousins that I refer to as "aunt" or "uncle" because they're closer in age to my grandparents than they are to me. I can't remember a family reunion without at least a hundred people in attendance. And those were just the cousins who lived locally. Whether it was a wedding, a birthday party or a Christmas potluck in my great-aunt Dorothy's garage, I could always count on there being a handful of cousins my age to hang out with.

When I found out that one of my favorite Montana Mavericks families, the Sanchezes of Bronco, had a set of cousins in the nearby town of Tenacity, I was so excited to "explore" this branch of the family tree and revisit a few of my most memorable characters.

Ever since she was a kid, Nina Sanchez knew she was going to marry Barrett Deroy, her brother's best friend. Just because Barrett and his parents mysteriously left town fifteen years ago doesn't mean Nina is willing to give up the dream. Or at least the dream of proving her childhood sweetheart's innocence. Luckily, Nina has the help of her great-uncle Stanley to find out what happened to the Deroys—and the town's missing money.

For more information on my other Harlequin Montana Mavericks and Special Edition books, visit my website at christyjeffries.com, or chat with me on X @christyjeffries. You can also find me on Facebook and Instagram. I'd love to hear from you.

Enjoy,

Christy Jeffries

THEIR MAVERICK SUMMER

CHRISTY JEFFRIES

MONTANA MAVERICKS

Special thanks and acknowledgment are given to Christy Jeffries for her contribution to the Montana Mavericks: The Tenacity Social Club miniseries.

Harlequin®
MONTANA MAVERICKS

Recycling programs for this product may not exist in your area.

ISBN-13: 978-1-335-14323-5

Their Maverick Summer

Copyright © 2025 by Harlequin Enterprises ULC

For questions and comments about the quality of this book, please contact us at CustomerService@Harlequin.com.

Harlequin Enterprises ULC
22 Adelaide St. West, 41st Floor
Toronto, Ontario M5H 4E3, Canada
www.Harlequin.com

Printed in Lithuania

MIX
Paper | Supporting responsible forestry
FSC® C021394

Christy Jeffries graduated from the University of California, Irvine, with a degree in criminology and received her Juris Doctor from California Western School of Law. But drafting court documents and working in law enforcement was merely an apprenticeship for her current career in the dynamic field of mommyhood and romance writing. Christy lives in Southern California with her patient husband, two sarcastic sons and a sweet husky who sheds appreciation all over her car and house.

Visit the Author Profile page
at Harlequin.com for more titles.

To Jessica Graham Philips, my best favorite cousin in the world. (It's okay, all the other cousins already know we're each other's favorite.) The first known photo of us "together" is a side-by-side of our moms with their pregnant bellies. From tea parties to two dollar you-call-its, you've always been my wingwoman. You even got a fake ID the same day I turned twenty-one so that I would never have to go out drinking (or line dancing) alone. And when we needed to haul a heavy, boxy TV upstairs into our first apartment together, you knew just who to call for reinforcements...which is how I met my future husband. Growing up with you was a blessing. But *becoming* a grown-up with you was even better. Sometimes I don't know how we made it out of early adulthood, but I can't imagine a better person to have by my side through every phase of my life.

I love you, Cousin...

Chapter One

Normally, Nina Sanchez loved summers in Tenacity, Montana. And she loved her great uncle even more. But if she didn't get a hold of Uncle Stanley real quick, the Fourth of July fireworks weren't going to be the only things exploding tonight.

Using the crumpled flyer from the hot dog–eating contest to fan her flushed face, she watched her octogenarian uncle and his bride of almost six months, Winona Cobbs-Sanchez, stand up on the small stage in the center of the town park and announce that they may have finally cracked the mystery of what happened with the Deroy family.

It would've been nice if Uncle Stanley had given Nina some advance notice before dropping this bombshell during the town festivities. Instead, Nina's mind had just been blown and her nerves now pinged with electrical currents. Yet she somehow managed to hold back a whole list of rapid-fire questions that had been haunting her for the past fifteen years.

A few of their neighbors, though, weren't quite as restrained.

"Who cares what happened to those no-good Deroys?" someone shouted from the crowd. Nina inwardly cringed at hearing the disparaging reference. Not that she hadn't heard it all before. "The town finally got the money back, and that's all that matters."

"Justice matters," someone else hollered. "We can't just let the Deroy boy get away with it."

"If you have proof that Barrett Deroy stole money from the town-renovation fund, Clovis, then you should probably share it with the authorities." Mrs. Vandergrift, the retired high school principal, still had the same trademark reprimanding tone.

Not many people had joined Nina in defending Barrett Deroy fifteen years ago. Of course, it would've been easier to defend Barrett if he and his parents hadn't disappeared right after the town's renovation fund went missing.

Nina reminded herself that there had to be a good reason her childhood sweetheart hadn't tried to contact her after suddenly leaving town under the most suspicious of circumstances. Maybe he'd died in a tragic accident. Or maybe he'd gone to prison. Or maybe he'd gotten married to a cheerleader from his college and had half a dozen kids by now.

Honestly, she wasn't sure which outcome would break her heart more.

Biting her lower lip, Nina scolded herself. Obviously, Barrett dying would be the worst-case scenario. But still. It hurt to think that someone she'd once thought of as her soul mate had moved on so quickly without giving her a second thought.

"All I know," Brent Woodson said, holding up a bottle of beer as if he was giving a toast, "is that if Barrett Deroy ever shows up in Tenacity again, we're going to finally get the chance to lock him up for what he did."

"You mean for what *your* family did?"

Nina didn't recognize the deep voice coming from the

crowd behind her, but she *did* recognize the way the skin on the back of her neck flushed with heat. Not having experienced the feeling in so long, she'd almost forgotten that there was only one person in the world who'd ever set off an immediate tingling sensation in her body simply by his presence.

Barrett Deroy.

Nina's head swiveled to find the boy she'd been looking for all these years. Instead, her eyes landed on a full-grown man striding purposely toward Brent Woodson, the former mayor's son.

Her mouth dropped open as she stared in disbelief.

Barrett was actually here. In Tenacity. Nina had played out this exact moment in her mind countless times, trying to imagine what he might look like now. She'd envisioned him fat, bald, possibly disguising himself behind a full beard or a pair of glasses. But the only changes to his appearance appeared to be four extra inches in height, about thirty more pounds of pure muscle, and a hardened jawline where his boyishly fuller cheeks used to be.

At least, his face seemed more chiseled from where she was standing, but it was too difficult to get a good view since the man weaved through the crowd just as quickly and effortlessly as he had when he scored the rushing touchdown in the state championship game his sophomore year.

Brent squared his chest just as Barrett stopped inches from him, the two former rivals suddenly face to face again.

"You have the audacity to show your face in *my* town and try to trash my family's good name?" Brent challenged. "Good luck doing that from a jail cell, Deroy."

"Don't tell me you still think you and your daddy own this town, Woodson." Barrett's tone was ice cold, and his stance was completely sober compared to Brent, who was swaying slightly in his stars-and-stripes swim trunks.

Nina didn't realize her feet were propelling her forward until she was inches from Barrett's side. The sweet, agreeable boy she'd once adored had been replaced by a more mature, guarded, and somewhat-bitter adult man. When had Barrett learned how to sneer like that?

Brent pulled back his fist, but before he could swing, Uncle Stanley had effortlessly hooked his arm around the younger man's waist and yanked him away from Barrett.

"That's enough of that, boys," the eighty-eight-year-old said casually, as if he broke up fights every day. "Save the drama for tomorrow. Tonight is for celebration."

As if to punctuate Uncle Stanley's commanding words, the first loud bang of fireworks exploded in the sky above them. But Barrett didn't bother to look up. His eyes had finally landed on Nina, who'd instinctively placed herself directly between him and Brent.

Now it was Barrett's turn to be surprised, and she watched the warring expressions cross his face: joy, anger, disappointment, confusion. His mouth opened, then closed. If Nina had been hoping for some sort of apology, she certainly wouldn't be able to hear it over the fireworks and the assembled crowd that was now oohing and aahing over the display in the night sky.

Instead of uttering so much as a greeting to Nina, though, Barrett abruptly turned and made his way back through the clusters of people.

Oh, hell no. Nina was not about to let him run away from her without an explanation. Not again.

"Barrett, wait!" Her feet sprang into action as she chased after him. It wasn't the first time she'd had to run to catch up with him.

He was closer in age to her big brother, Luca, and growing up, Nina had been the kid sister always following them around. Barrett, though, had been an only child and never seemed to mind hanging around all five of the Sanchez siblings. In fact, he often preferred spending time at their busy house than at his own down the street. When he and Luca would take off on their bikes for some grand adventure, Barrett would always be the first to slow down to allow Nina to tag along.

When Nina was several feet behind him, she called out again for him to stop but got no response. He must not have heard her over the barking labradoodle wearing a red, white, and blue bandana. The dog's owner seemed to be struggling with their decision to bring a young pup to a fireworks show. But at least the threat of getting tangled up in Corky's leash slowed Barrett long enough for Nina to catch up.

Nina grabbed Barrett's upper arm to get his attention, then gasped in shock not only at her forwardness but also at the fact that the once-familiar arm of an athletic teen was now the muscular bicep of a grown man.

So much had changed in fifteen years. Maybe it would have been better to only think about him in her memories, to only remember how they used to be. Suddenly, she wasn't so sure that she wanted any answers at all.

Barrett glanced at Nina's fingers right below the cuff of his T-shirt. He didn't yank his arm away, but he also didn't give her a welcoming smile. Or any smile at all. He barely lifted his eyes to hers before quickly shifting his attention to a spot somewhere in the distance. "I think my coming back here might have been a mistake."

Nina swallowed a lump of disappointment at the first words he finally said to her after all these years apart. So far, this wasn't proving to be the happy reunion she'd imagined in her dreams. But she had to at least try. "I'm glad you're here, Barrett. It's good to see you."

Finally, his gaze met hers. Those piercing brown eyes were still as penetrating as ever, and she stood still, allowing him to study her for several moments. She blinked twice in a row and then a third time when she thought she saw the corner of his mouth tilt slightly upward. Was he… smirking at her?

Barrett released a long breath. "You never could beat me in a staring contest, Nina Sanchez."

"Well, you've grown a couple of inches since the last time we had one, Barrett Deroy. But at least you still remember my name." It was the closest she dared come to chastising him for his abrupt departure from her life.

Instead of getting defensive like he had been in the crowded park, he simply nodded. "I deserve that. I didn't think we'd ever see each other again. I'm sorry for the way I had to leave."

Now *this* was more along the lines of what she'd been envisioning as far as reunions went. The apology was a start, but she was still hoping for an explanation.

"I didn't understand it at the time. Not that I understand it any better now." Nina smiled, relieved that she didn't have to force it. "But I'm really glad you're here."

"What?" Barrett said, pointing to his ear as another round of fireworks exploded and a baby in a nearby stroller started crying.

Clearly, they weren't going to have much of a conversation unless they either yelled or waited until the park cleared out. Nina, who still hadn't released his arm, tugged him forward and hoped he could read her lips when she shouted, "Let's go this way so we can talk."

* * *

It wasn't as though Barrett Deroy had expected the town of Tenacity to welcome him back with open arms. The past fifteen years had quickly taught him to be a realist and manage his expectations. So when his former girlfriend dragged him toward the small parking lot behind the Grizzly Bar, his first assumption was that Nina Sanchez didn't want to be seen in public with him. It was why he'd initially tried to move away from the crowd so quickly. He didn't want to see the hurt or the accusations in her pretty brown eyes.

But then Nina caught up to him and forced him to turn around. He hadn't been able to look away. He made the stupid joke about their old staring contests so that he wouldn't accidentally blurt out that she was even more beautiful than he'd remembered.

Nina Sanchez had grown into quite a woman. A strong and determined woman, judging by the way she'd managed to grab onto him when he was storming away. But also quite stunning. Especially since the soft touch of her hand still felt exactly the same. How easily he'd just allowed her to steer him down a dark alley toward the back of a brick building.

Then again, she'd always tried to steer him wherever she wanted, ever since they were in grade school.

She opened her mouth to speak, then paused as the final crescendo of fireworks culminated in a finale of pops and bangs. They both looked up at the sky to watch, neither one of them talking or moving for several moments. Besides their strong physical connection, they'd also always shared a mental connection that made it easy to comfortably be quiet in each other's presence.

Smoke was still in the air when Nina took a deep breath

and released it with a sigh. "Do you remember the last time we spent Fourth of July together?"

For the first time in days, Barrett felt his lips pull into a slight grin. Fifteen years ago, they'd ditched their families and friends in the town park and gone off to the woods for a serious make-out session.

"I remember feeling like we were so invincible, like we were on top of the world with our plans for the future and how easy life was going to be for us once we got mar—" He shook his head to clear the image of Nina in a wedding gown. "But we were just kids back then, weren't we? I grew up fast after that."

"We *both* grew up fast," Nina corrected him. Her tone didn't exactly sound like she was blaming him, but he'd been blaming himself for so long that his defenses rose to the surface.

"At least you got to stay in the place you loved." He stopped himself from making any other assumptions about what her life had been like after he'd left. He'd purposely avoided searching for her online because he hadn't wanted to see how happy she ended up once she'd moved on from him.

"Where did you guys go anyway?" Nina asked.

It was such a simple question and one that he'd actually anticipated. Yet he'd been on guard for so many years, being so careful not to give anyone too much information, it felt like he was betraying his parents by finally talking about it.

He let his shoulders roll back, trying to release the weight of a long-buried secret. "We bounced around a little bit at first, staying at dive motels like fugitives on the run. We ended up settling in Whitehorn, but not until my parents changed our names."

"You changed your names?" When she said it like that, it did seem rather incredulous.

"I guess they didn't want to be found." He shrugged away the protectiveness creeping back into his shoulders.

"Well, they certainly did a good job of that, because I looked all over for you."

"You looked for me?" Maybe she hadn't moved on as easily as he'd assumed. Or maybe she'd simply been searching for the missing money everyone else had accused him of stealing.

"I mean, I wasn't legally driving at first, so I couldn't actively track you or anything. And we only had the one computer at home that all of us kids had to share. I tried out my online-sleuthing skills at the school library, but you know how closely those devices were monitored. Social media was still relatively new back then, so I followed the accounts of most of the high schools in Montana, thinking I might catch a glimpse of you on the field or some sort of clue. Later, I pored over the stats of your favorite college teams, hoping you were still playing football somewhere."

Barrett's throat grew tight, and he resisted the urge to tug at his collar. "Actually, I stopped playing after leaving Tenacity."

"But you loved football. There's no way you wouldn't have made the varsity team somewhere else. Did you get hurt?"

Not unless he counted heartbreak as being hurt.

"It just seemed pointless with everything else going on. Like a luxury that we couldn't afford. In fact, my parents made me get my GED because they were worried about having my transcripts transferred to another high school." He lifted his chin higher. "But the bright side is that I was able to get a jump on classes at the community college."

It also gave him extra time to work and pay his tuition since he was determined to get a degree from a four-year university despite realizing he wasn't going to land the athletic scholarship everyone had always assumed was a sure thing.

Nina frowned. "That's a lot of effort to keep a low profile. And a whole helluva lot to give up. Why would your parents put you—and themselves—through all of that over some speculation that never amounted to more than petty gossip?"

"Petty gossip? Mayor Woodson told my dad that I was the number one suspect and that the sheriff had enough evidence to throw me in juvenile hall."

"But running away only made you look more guilty."

"Maybe my parents believed I was."

Nina gasped. "Nobody who truly knows you, Barrett, would think that you actually stole the money. Your parents obviously loved you enough to uproot their entire lives. I'm just trying to figure out what would drive them to do something so rash."

"Jeez, Nina. You clearly still have a thing for playing detective." He ran his hand through his hair. "This is starting to sound like an interrogation. Are you sure you're not carrying a badge in the back pocket of those shorts?"

"No, I just listen to a lot of true crime podcasts. And why are you frowning at my shorts?" She smoothed her hands against her hips, which only served to draw his attention to the exact part of her body he'd been trying not to stare at. "They're the same cutoffs I've been wearing since eighth grade."

"Well, your legs have gotten a couple inches longer since then." His voice sounded raspy to his own ears, and he crossed his arms in front of his chest so that he could prevent his hands from following the same path hers had just taken.

It was dark in the parking lot, but the light shining over the back door to the Grizzly Bar gave off enough glow to reveal the rosy blush now coloring Nina's cheeks. Did she know what being this close to her was doing to him?

"All I'm saying, Barrett, is that I couldn't imagine ever being able to give up the name *Sanchez* and start a new life somewhere else. Something must have made your parents do what they did."

Apparently, Nina hadn't only gotten more attractive with time, she'd also gotten more persistent. He might as well tell her what he knew. If they just stood here staring at each other, he would be way too tempted to pull her into his arms.

"I'm not exactly sure what went down," he said honestly. "Somehow, someone concocted evidence to make it look like I stole thousands of dollars from the Tenacity-restoration fund. I don't know if the mayor was the first one to suggest that it was me or if he was only the messenger telling my parents that I was a suspect. But once my name was out there, nobody seemed to care about motive. I have no idea why my parents didn't try to fight it. Maybe they thought that no attorney would be able to combat the powerful Woodsons. Maybe they thought my reputation would be tarnished regardless, which it obviously was. All I know was that they woke me up in the middle of the night and told me we were leaving town. They wouldn't even let me write a note to say goodbye to you. My dad said anyone I contacted might be considered an accomplice."

"I can still remember everything about the day I found out you were gone." Nina's eyes closed, and she sniffed before opening them again. "It was the worst day of my life."

Guilt gripped his chest, and he fought the urge to pull her into his arms and tell her that he was there to make everything better. He rocked back on his heels, knowing that she deserved better than hearing a promise he wasn't sure that he could keep.

"I'm sorry things happened the way they did. I felt so powerless, like I was being dragged away from everything I knew. From everyone I lo—" He stopped himself before he said the *L* word. "The only thing I had control over was keeping you out of the mess. I didn't want anyone thinking you were somehow involved. My parents tried to protect me, and I tried to protect you."

Nina looked away from him and shook her head.

Instead of trying to make her understand, his heart simply sank. "You don't believe me."

Her eyes snapped back to his. "Of course I believe you. I've always believed in you, Barrett. I wasn't shaking my head because I doubted you. I was shaking my head because your protection was misguided. It was all for nothing."

"What do you mean?"

"When you left the way you did, so many kids at school were saying that you were a thief, including half the football team."

"I'm surprised it was just half," he said.

"Well, a lot of guys had their hearts set on returning to the state championship that season you left. Tenacity High hasn't even made it to the regional playoffs since then, and that might've been a bigger betrayal to the town than the missing funds. People got bitter. One of Brent Woodson's buddies openly accused me of being your lookout and covering for you."

Barrett grimaced. It was the exact thing he'd hoped to

avoid, the only reason he'd stayed away all this time. Yet it had happened anyway. "I'm so sorry, Nina."

Nina dragged in a deep breath and exhaled. Something about being in her presence made him feel as though he could finally breathe again, too.

Several tension-filled seconds passed between them before she finally offered him a guarded smile. He didn't blame her for not trusting him or his motives for returning. But at least she was still standing here, willing to hear his side of the story. Unfortunately, he'd never really known what his side of the story was.

Chapter Two

"Tell me what your life is like now," Nina prompted, still standing way too close to him.

Barrett wanted to tell her everything, but he'd been living under the radar for so long, keeping his past a secret, he didn't know how to open up to anyone anymore. Most people were satisfied with vague answers, but he had a feeling Nina wouldn't be appeased until she found out everything she could.

"I own a small horse ranch outside of Whitehorn," he offered before doing what he usually did during conversations—turn the focus back to the other person. "What about you? How's your family?"

"They're good. Dad is still farming. Mom is still sewing. She finally opened her own little shop and even does classes once a month at the Tenacity Quilting Club. Diego and Julian are both engaged, and my sister, Marisa, got married and moved to Bronco. My mom doesn't think Luca will ever find someone since he's always working. Although she probably says the same thing about me whenever I have to stay late at a ranch."

"A ranch?" His forehead rose. "As in multiple ranches?"

"I train horses to work with cattle. Some of the bigger ranches can afford to have a trainer on staff. But Tenacity and most of the counties around here have smaller ranches and can only afford to get new horses every so often. They usually don't have the manpower or time to get an untrained horse up to speed without slowing down the rest of their cattle operations. I go where I'm needed, spend a few weeks working with a horse or two, then move on to the next horse, the next ranch. Currently, I'm at Forrester Farms in town, so it's easy enough for me to stay put at my parents' place this summer. But obviously, the goal would be to one day have my own small spread where people could bring their horses to me."

"Wait. You don't live with anyone? Does that mean you never married?" Barrett suddenly wanted to know if she ever came close.

"You make it sound like I'm some sort of old maid. Or that my marriage years are far behind me. I'm only twenty-nine, Barrett."

He looked at the date on his watch. "Actually, you'll be thirty in two days. Does your mom still make you a strawberry cake every year for your birthday?"

One side of Nina's mouth lifted in an adorable half grin. "I guess you'll have to stay in town long enough to find out."

She probably remembered that he had always been a sucker for Mrs. Sanchez's baked goods.

"As of right now, I don't know how long I plan to stay." He wanted to keep his guard up, but he'd also always been a sucker for Nina's flirtatious smile. Plus, he was increasingly curious about her relationship status. "Don't singles in Tenacity go on the dating apps?"

"As a matter of fact, they do. If you're looking for that sort of thing. Although, I should warn you that if ever need to leave an awkward date, we don't have Uber yet. The closest thing we have for a ride-sharing service is the Tenacity

Shuttler. And that's only when Cecil Brewster isn't at the quilting club or watching Jeopardy. He never misses either."

"Cecil, the old cowboy who held national rodeo titles for steer wrestling, is a quilter?"

"He's more of a gossiper than a quilter, but I heard his running stitch is getting better."

Barrett chuckled. "Well, I drove my own truck, so I don't need a rideshare. And I definitely wasn't looking for a match on a dating app. It was more of a joke to find out why you're still single."

"Oh." The blush returned to her cheeks. "I've actually met a couple of guys that way. Obviously after making sure they weren't, in fact, serial killers. Not that I'm actively looking now. Or even then. I'm usually too busy working to date much. There was a time in my early twenties when I had to face reality and get the memory of you out of my head, and it seemed easy enough to date somebody short-term because my job kept me moving from ranch to ranch. But I already know almost everyone in town and there's never been anyone I could imagine building a future with."

He wanted to ask her what she meant when she said she had to get the memory of him out of her head. But the truth was that if she was anything like him, he already knew. He'd done the exact same thing trying to get over her. He cleared his throat and asked, "So you're an almost thirty-year-old spinster?"

Her eyes widened, and he quickly held up his palms. "I didn't mean that the way it sounded. I'm just surprised nobody has snatched you up yet."

She put her hands on her hips. "I don't see a ring on your finger either, pal. I'm guessing there isn't a Mrs. Deroy?"

Hearing his real name on her lips was almost more than he could handle.

"No, there's not a Mrs. Deroy. There's not even a Mrs. Jones."

"Jones?" she asked.

"Yeah, my parents weren't too original when they picked Barry Jones as my alias."

"Barry?" Nina scrunched her nose. "You hated it when people use to call you Barry."

"I still do. Which is why I go by B.D. Jones nowadays. Although I've enjoyed hearing you say *Barrett* tonight." As soon as he made the admission, he knew he shouldn't have opened that door. He didn't need to be giving anyone false hope. Especially himself. "Anyway, when it came to dating, I never let it get to the relationship stage. How could I make a commitment to someone when I couldn't even tell them my real name?"

She studied him for several moments, and he stood there, letting her. Clearly, she was just as curious about him as he had been about her. But if he truly wanted to move on from the past, he had to let go of his old dreams. He had to let go of the idea of him and Nina together again.

Finally, she spoke. "So what do your parents think about you returning to the scene of the crime?"

"Not only did they not want me to come, they flipped out when I told them. My mom locked herself in her bedroom for hours, doing whatever she does when she doesn't want to deal with things. My dad said they'd spent years trying to start a new life and accused me of trying to ruin it all."

"I suppose I could understand their concern. Even at sixteen, you could have been charged as an adult. But hasn't the statute of limitations run out by now?"

"I actually asked a friend of mine who used to be a cop. He said the Montana statute of limitations is ten years, but since I might have been considered actively evasive, the clock wouldn't have started running. But the bigger point is that I'm not guilty of anything and I need to do whatever it takes to prove that."

"Did the cops ever question you back then?"

"Nope. Only Mayor Woodson, who said the sheriff planned to arrest me." It had seemed like a much scarier prospect as a sixteen-year-old since Barrett hadn't known that he could've tried to fight the charges. "As far as I know, we left before they could start their investigation."

"But weren't you worried that you were making it worse by leaving?" Nina asked.

"I was terrified for all of us. I felt like a fugitive those first few years, always looking over my shoulder and flinching every time I heard a siren or saw a cop car. But after a while, I realized that I'd given my thumbprint when I got my driver's license and I used my same Social Security number when I opened an account at the bank. See, my parents legally changed our names, but they never bothered to get me a new identification. Eventually, it became more apparent that if there had ever been an actual warrant for my arrest, the cops would've shown up by now. It just became less of a hassle to keep doing what I'd always done."

"So, then, what made you change your mind?" she asked. "What made you decide to finally come back to Tenacity?"

"Your uncle Stanley and Winona. They came out to my ranch looking for me and said the missing money had been found under some big rock off Juniper Road. My neighbor is a retired NYPD detective and called in a favor. He confirmed that there'd never been a warrant issued for Barrett Deroy."

"Well, I could've told you that much." Nina rolled her pretty brown eyes as if she already had everything figured out and he was the last one to know.

"You always did like solving a mystery and cracking the case."

"It wasn't so much that I solved anything. I just happened to have dat...known someone in law enforcement and asked him to run your name."

Barrett had a feeling she'd been about to say that she'd dated a cop, which would have been the second time she'd dropped the hint that she'd moved on with her life since they were teenagers. They both had.

Knowing that he wasn't a wanted man and wouldn't be putting Nina in any jeopardy was the only reason why he'd agreed to return to Tenacity. He shrugged. "I guess you could say I was ready to face the past and put it behind me once and for all."

Nina studied him, but Barrett was much harder to read now than he'd been when they were happy and carefree kids. She wanted to ask him if she was included in the past he was hoping to put behind him. But it was way too soon for all that.

Her feet grew restless, and she was ready to finally put the next phase of her plan in motion. "The first thing we should probably do is get you a good attorney."

Barrett lifted one eyebrow. "We?"

"We always worked well together. Remember that time we found out who was writing those horrible things about Coach Parker on the stalls in the school bathroom? You thought it was another kid pulling a prank, but I told you the handwriting looked like an adult trying write like a student."

Barrett's exhale sounded like a sigh. "I missed two afternoons of football practice to hide out in that tiny custodian closet across the hall only to find out it was Miss DeMato, who was mad that Coach dumped her before they were supposed to chaperone the winter formal together. Whatever happened to Miss DeMato?"

"She's Mrs. Parker now."

"Coach married her after all that drama?"

"No. But his brother did. They moved to Kalispell, last I heard. It was quite a scandal and got people in Tenacity talking about something other than the Deroys."

As soon as the words were out of her mouth, Nina wished she could take them back. She shouldn't have reminded him about his family being the subject of gossip.

Barrett frowned again. "My situation isn't some love story gone bad, though, Nina. I don't want you mixed up in any of this. I never wanted my trouble to touch you or your family."

"Except I'm already involved, Barrett." Having three older brothers and a handful of male cousins, Nina was accustomed to overprotective guys. One of the things she'd always appreciated about Barrett, though, was that he didn't treat her like a kid sister. Or at least he hadn't before now. "I'm the one who recruited Uncle Stanley to try to find you. I'm the one who has been pushing to clear your name. Let me help."

"Fine." He crossed his arms in front of him. "But I already hired an attorney."

"Good. They can deal with speaking to the authorities on your behalf while you and I start figuring out who had a motive to steal the town's money."

"Or who had a motive to frame me."

Nina tilted her head. "Who would want to make you look bad? Everyone in town loved you. Or at least they used to back then."

"Not everyone." Barrett jerked a thumb toward the town park, which was emptying out now that the fireworks were over. "You heard Brent Woodson back there. There's never been any love lost between the two of us."

"You two seemed to get along fine when we were kids. I never understood how it turned into such a rivalry in high school."

Brent had been the town's golden child who had always gotten anything he wanted as if it was his birthright. Barrett, on the other hand, was the son of a horse farrier and a grocery-store checker, both of whom worked extra hours to put food on the table.

"Because no matter how much Woodson's parents spoiled him, I had something that he didn't."

"I guess you're right." Nina's nose wrinkled slightly. "He never liked being second best when it came to football."

"Nina," Barrett said simply, then shook his head as though he had to explain something to a clueless child. "Brent's jealousy wasn't just on the field. He wanted my girlfriend, too."

Her eyes went wide. "Me? Why would he want me when he was dating…" She paused as things began to click into place.

"How could you have not known? I thought for sure Brent would've tried to take my place the second I was gone."

"Well, back then I never gave him much thought. I still don't. But now that you mention it, one time, at the Social Club, he told me that if I needed a shoulder to cry on, he was there for me. Although, I had so many other things on my mind back then that even if he was trying to 'comfort me'—" Nina used two fingers to make quotation marks in the air "—I wouldn't have picked up on it."

Barrett muttered something under his breath, but Nina's ears perked up when she distinctly heard the words "punch" and "smug face."

The last thing she needed right now was a couple of grown men reliving some petty schoolyard quarrel. So she redirected his attention by asking, "But would teenage jealousy really have been motive enough?"

"Maybe," Barrett offered.

"Did he have opportunity, though? If I remember correctly, his dad sent him to that NFL player's training camp the summer it happened. Wait. Weren't you supposed to go to that camp with him?"

"I was." Barrett's arms were still crossed in front of his chest. "It was super expensive, and you helped me apply for a scholarship since there was no way my parents could afford it. But my dad was going to be out of town for work again and my mom hated staying alone at night."

"That's right." Maybe if Barrett had gone to that football camp, he wouldn't have been a suspect either. Instead of pointing out the obvious, she said, "See, this is the kind of stuff you and I can work on piecing together. Where are you staying while you're in town?"

He took a step back, as though he was going to bolt again. "I booked a room at the Tenacity Inn for the time being. Why?"

"Because you have a habit of disappearing and I want to know where to find you."

Dale Clutterbuck, the big, bearded bartender and owner of the Grizzly Bar, stepped into the parking lot with a full black trash bag. He paused as he took in the sight of a woman alone with a man in a dark parking lot behind the bar. "Everything okay back here?"

"Yep, Dale. Just a couple of old friends catching up. Do you remember Barrett Deroy?"

"Deroy?" Dale asked, then squinted. "Oh yeah. You look just like your old man."

"I get that a lot," Barrett said even though the observation didn't exactly sound like a compliment. Personally, Nina didn't see the resemblance, but it wasn't like she had a clear memory of what Mr. Deroy had looked like. Even if he hadn't traveled for work all the time, Barrett used to spend more time with the Sanchez family than she ever had with his.

"We should probably head back," Nina said, looping her hand through the crook of Barrett's arm. She used her free hand to wave at the bartender as she started walking toward the main street. "See you later, Dale."

Nina paused where the side alley opened up and looked both ways before continuing on the busy sidewalk. But when she resumed her pace, she realized she was suddenly pulling on an immovable object, her hand wedged tightly between Barrett's bicep and his rib cage.

Her eyes traveled up to find him staring down at her. She hoped that was a smirk on his mouth.

"You don't have to perp walk me," he told her. "I'm not going to take off running or try to escape. Like I said, I want to get this resolved once and for all so that I can get back to my normal life."

Right. Tenacity wasn't his normal life. Nina wasn't his normal life, either. He would only be here temporarily.

She yanked her hand away, effectively setting him free. But she wasn't ready to lose all connection with him again. "Do you have a phone?"

"I haven't been hiding out in a cave all these years, Nina. Of course I have a phone." He pulled it out of the front pocket of his jeans to prove it.

"Can I see it?" She held out her hand.

"If this is what it takes to establish trust." He placed his phone in her palm. She almost shoved it back at him, not liking the implication that she was being insecure. Then he said, "The passcode is 0706."

Her breath caught in her throat, and she blinked several times. "You used my birthday as your passcode?"

"It's an easy number to remember." His explanation sounded reasonable enough, but he didn't meet her eyes.

She dropped her gaze to focus on his phone, trying to keep her fingers steady as she typed in her contact information. As soon as she handed his device back to him, a ping came from her back pocket. She retrieved her own phone and showed him the notification of the text message she'd just sent herself. "Now I have your number, too, just in case."

"In case I skip town again?" There was a hint of playfulness in his tone. "Did you want to walk back to the hotel with me to confirm that I'm actually staying there?"

"No need." She swiped up on her screen to show him the next text-message notification.

It was from Carol Overton, the front desk clerk at the Tenacity Inn.

You'll never believe who checked in an hour ago. I didn't recognize the name on the reservation because he might be using an alias. But he looks just like his dad.

While he was reading, another text notification popped up on her screen, followed by several more.

"So much for keeping a low profile," he muttered.

"To be fair, you kind of blew your own cover when you confronted Brent Woodson during the biggest event in town." She returned her phone to her back pocket as the pinging sounds continued. "When do you meet with your attorney?"

He ran his fingers through his hair. "Tomorrow morning at ten."

"Good. We can grab breakfast at the Silver Spur Café beforehand. I'll bring my notes."

"You have notes?" he asked.

"You may not have talked to me for the past fifteen years, Barrett, but don't act like you don't know me."

With that, Nina walked away first this time.

His room at the Tenacity Inn was comfortable enough, but Barrett's mind was racing too fast to fall asleep. He thought about the missing money, he thought about his parents' concern over him coming back to a place they'd left in disgrace, he thought about how the townspeople were already reacting to his return.

But mostly, he thought about Nina Sanchez.

He didn't bother to tell her that he hadn't invited her to his meeting with the attorney. It would've been pointless anyway. Clearly, Nina was still just as tenacious as the town she'd been raised in. The woman who'd confidently stood before him a few hours ago was no different than the girl he used to know.

What she hadn't seemed to figure out, though, was that Barrett was no longer the same easygoing kid. Leaving Tenacity had forced him to grow up quickly, and he no longer dreamt of football and teenage crushes and Mrs. Sanchez's strawberry cake.

Okay, so maybe once in a while he thought about those things—especially the strawberry cake. However, he never allowed himself to dwell on what he couldn't have. Which was probably why he tossed and turned all night in the hotel bed. Every time his mind wandered down the road of what could have been, he would have to mentally yank himself back to the present.

When the sun rose the following morning, he still didn't have any answers about why the people of Tenacity had made him out to be the villain. Stanley Sanchez had explained that the missing money had already been found and was back in town's coffers. So why the grudge?

Clearly, there was more to the story than what he'd understood at the naive age of sixteen. As he stepped into the shower, he reminded himself that it didn't matter what the rest of the story was. All that mattered was that he cleared his family's name once and for all.

He checked his email and saw that his attorney's office wasn't set up yet, as the man was new to Tenacity. The attorney suggested getting together for breakfast instead, and Barrett had to wonder if Nina had somehow orchestrated this as well. When Barrett arrived at the Silver Spur Café ten minutes early, he wasn't surprised to see her already there in a corner booth with an open laptop and two mugs of steaming-hot coffee.

"I wasn't sure if you still used cream and sugar," she explained when she passed him a menu. "I didn't want to make any assumptions."

Oh, so now she didn't want to make assumptions. After she'd already assumed that he would welcome her help at this meeting with his attorney. But Barrett kept his thoughts to himself. After all, it wasn't her fault he hadn't had a decent night's sleep.

"Hey, Nina," a young man in a cowboy hat said as he stopped by their table. "Bruiser's been doing much better with the smaller calves since you worked with him using those leg cues."

"Oh, hey, Ryan." Nina barely glanced up from dumping

eight packets of sugar into her coffee. "I'm glad we got him to stop nipping them. Make sure he sees your rope swinging out toward the herd occasionally so he remembers that *you're* in charge of redirecting the stragglers, not him."

"Maybe if you get a chance, you could stop by the ranch and see how he's doing. I know Bruiser's been missing you."

Barrett fought the urge to roll his eyes. Whoever Ryan was, he seemed oblivious to the fact that another man was sitting at the same table as Nina. The young pup clearly only had eyes for her as he stood there, shifting from one boot to the other. More like Ryan was the one missing Nina being out on his ranch.

"That rope trick sounds like the method my dad showed us when he was shoeing horses," Barrett said, finally drawing the newcomer's attention his way. "Moving the tools in and out of their peripheral view so they get accustomed to being around working humans."

"I don't remember much about your dad, Barrett." Nina finally looked up from her over-sweetened mug of coffee, a smile on her face. "But I do remember that bit of advice. Mr. Deroy did have a way with horses."

"Deroy? As in *the* Barrett Deroy? The one Uncle Clovis says stole the…" The younger man trailed off as Barrett narrowed his eyes, practically daring him to finish the accusation.

"Ryan," Nina said, saving everyone from the awkwardness. "This is my friend, Barrett Deroy. We grew up together. He's back in Tenacity to clear up some unfinished business. Right now our schedule is pretty full, but if we get a free moment, maybe I'll bring him by the ranch to say hi to your uncle. Barrett, you remember Clovis Peck, don't you? This is his nephew, Ryan."

Barrett would have chuckled at Nina's obvious attempt to oversell his innocence if he wasn't so flattered by it. By publicly acknowledging their friendship and implying that they were working together, she was effectively putting the townspeople on notice that she was on Team Deroy. Man, he forgot how good it felt to have Nina in his corner.

"Nice to meet you." Ryan reached out, and Barrett accepted the handshake. "Any *friend* of Nina's is a friend of mine."

"Likewise," Barrett responded. He'd heard the emphasis on the word *friend* and didn't mind the fact that he was being sized up as a potential rival for Nina's affection. Probably because Nina wasn't showing an ounce of interest in the young man. She was already scanning the laminated menu, which she likely had memorized considering there weren't many other eating establishments in the small town.

At least Ryan knew when it was time to cut his losses and he said goodbye before picking up a to-go bag from the counter.

"You want to split the Belgian waffle, Barrett?" Nina asked. One of her most appealing qualities was that she had no clue how other guys saw her. He'd expected her to realize it once she'd gotten older and had more experience in the world. But clearly, she still hadn't caught on.

"The last time we split a waffle, you ate most of it."

She rolled her eyes. "We can get an extra plate and you can keep your half on that side of the table, out of my reach."

"Depends on if you want it with pecans or with chocolate chips."

"Why can't we get both?" She batted her pretty brown eyes at him, and he already knew he was going to be picking nuts out of his waffle.

Chapter Three

Nina had been ready to order as soon as she'd walked into the Silver Spur Café. But she didn't want to be shoving her face full of food when Barrett's attorney arrived. Thankfully, she didn't have to wait long.

"Is that your attorney?" Nina used her coffee mug to gesture outside the window toward a man exiting a nondescript white sedan.

"How can you tell?" Barrett asked.

"He's the only thirty-year-old in town wearing pressed khakis and a striped polo shirt this early on a Saturday morning. Since we don't have a golf course or a yacht club in Tenacity, it's a safe guess that he's not from around here."

Barrett stood up when the attorney entered the restaurant, but he didn't need to do anything else to draw the man's attention. Or anyone else's. Nina had forgotten how commanding Barrett's presence could be under normal circumstances. But with all the rumors surrounding his sudden return, nobody bothered to hide the fact that all eyes were on him.

After the men shook hands, Barrett introduced Nina to Marshall Gordon. "Marshall's grandfather owns the ranch next to mine in Whitehorn. He's the retired NYPD detective I was telling you about."

"Are you from New York also, Mr. Gordon?" Nina asked, even though she already knew the answer before she heard the attorney's East Coast accent.

"Please call me Marshall," he said as he slid into the booth across from her and set his laptop case in the same spot where Barrett had just been sitting. "Is it that obvious that I just moved here?"

Barrett didn't seem to mind that the attorney had commandeered his seat. Without saying a word, he sat on the vinyl bench next to Nina as if it was the most natural thing in the world. And fifteen years ago, it would have been.

To keep herself from focusing on the scent of Barrett's aftershave and the warmth of his body this close to hers, Nina tried to pay attention to what the newcomer was saying about the moving company losing some of his boxes, including the ones containing most of his clothes. "My grandpa said I was going to need some new threads to fit in here anyway, so I guess my next stop will be the nearest department store."

"The nearest department store is over an hour away in Bronco," Barrett said. "There are two feed-and-grain stores in town that probably carry a decent selection of jeans, work shirts, and boots. But you might want something a little more appropriate for the courtroom."

"Well, let's hope that I don't need to make a court appearance anytime soon." Marshall smiled. "Nina, I hope you aren't put off by the fact that I'm not from around here. All it took was one visit to my grandfather's ranch in Whitehorn, and I knew that the wide open spaces life was for me. Unfortunately, Gramps warned me that some of the locals won't be very receptive of a big-city transplant like myself."

"I hate to say that your grandfather might be right when it comes to a few of the locals," Nina admitted before passing Marshall a menu. "But I'm sure you'll find that most of the people in Tenacity are pretty friendly and welcoming. Personally, I think it's better for Barrett that you're not from around here."

"Oh yeah?" Marshall's brows rose over the frame of his glasses. "Why's that?"

"Because you'll be able to look at things with a fresh view."

"So you think that people have already made up their minds about—" Before Marshall could finish his question, raised voices from the kitchen interrupted him.

"I don't care if you fire me, Roger," the waitress who'd originally brought over the two cups of coffee prior to Barrett's arrival loudly told the cook. "I'm not serving that man. Not after my parents lost their bakery because of him."

Nina felt Barrett tense beside her. But she gave him credit for not making a bigger scene by getting up and leaving. She also gave herself credit for not telling Jocelyn Evans that her parents' failure to pay their insurance premiums, and not Barrett, was the reason why they hadn't been able to rebuild their bakery after the oven fire.

Instead, Nina lowered her voice. "Let's just say that when businesses went under after the renovation funds went missing, people wanted someone to blame. It was easy for them to buy into the rumors, no matter how unfounded they were."

"Sorry 'bout the wait, folks." The other waitress on duty pulled a pencil from behind her bun as she walked to their table. "What can I get you?"

"Thanks, Eileen." Nina smiled at the woman. "I'll take the country skillet with the eggs over easy and a side of biscuits and gravy."

"I thought we were sharing a waffle?" Barrett spoke quietly out the side of his mouth.

"We are. But since you're worried about me eating it all, I'm getting an appetizer to go with it." Nina handed Eileen her menu. "We'll also split the chocolate-pecan waffle with extra whipped cream."

"Two plates," Barrett added. "And an orange juice please."

When Eileen turned to Marshall, he blinked a couple of times before saying, "I'll…uh…just take the fruit cup."

"You must be new in town, huh?" The older waitress finished writing on her pad and then shoved her pencil back into her bun. "Don't worry. You can try to win the free T-shirt next time."

"The free what?" Marshall asked.

"The Silver Spur Challenge." Barrett pointed to the bottom of Marshall's menu. "It's one of those huge meals that are nearly impossible to finish, but if you do eat it all, you get a free shirt."

Marshall's expression looked slightly horrified, but he nodded politely. "I'll just stick with my fruit cup."

Eileen chuckled as she walked away.

Marshall pulled his laptop out of his bag and opened it on the table. "So I did some preliminary research and put in a request for any public records or reports filed with the county sheriff's office. They emailed me the initial report filed by the city clerk's office when the money went missing. The report is about as bare bones as it gets and doesn't mention any suspects or really any relevant information at all. It almost reads like an insurance claim. See?"

When Marshall turned the screen toward them, Nina had to lean in closer to Barrett so she could read with him. She was too focused on the words to think about the fact that their heads were only an inch apart.

"That's it?" Barrett asked when he finished reading the report. "It's barely two paragraphs."

"Right." Marshall moved the laptop back in front of him. "Now, there could be more info somewhere. Like a case file with notes not available to the public. Although I doubt the sheriff's office will share any unofficial files with me from the investigation—if there even was an investigation in the first place. Barrett, you said they never questioned you?"

"Nope. My parents only told me that the mayor talked to my dad and that Woodson was the one who pointed the finger at me."

"That's the part I'm stuck on." Marshall tapped the keyboard. "I don't want to make any presumptions about the former mayor or the city of Tenacity, but it would seem to me that if a well-respected mayor was advocating so hard to accuse you, Barrett, he would've had the authority and all of the town's resources to pursue charges. Yet as far as I can tell, he never did. There's not even a hint of your name in the initial report. I also checked the local newspaper articles around that time, and you're mentioned in the sports sections, but nothing linking you to the theft. That tells me that the newspapers didn't have any sufficient evidence either. Or at least nothing that could prevent them from getting hit with a libel suit."

Nina made a mental note to ask her mom if she remembered who used to run the *Tenacity Tribune* before they eventually shut down.

"Mayor Woodson was never the type to pick a losing side." She pushed up her sleeves, ready to dive right into the possibility of a grand conspiracy. "Maybe he already knew what the outcome would be."

Marshall seemed to consider her words, then continued.

"I'm also curious why your parents decided to leave town rather than confront their son's accusers."

Nina pointed a finger triumphantly. "Thank you! I've been saying the same thing for fifteen years."

Eileen brought their food, setting the personal-sized cast-iron skillet in front of Nina. She had to move her coffee to make room for the biscuits and the plate for her half of the waffle.

Marshall's eyes widened as he stared at the dishes now surrounding her. He opened his mouth, as if to make a comment, but apparently thought better of it.

"Roger says you're not getting another free T-shirt this month." The waitress jerked her thumb toward the wall of fame where Nina's photo had been on display for the past ten years. "I told him they don't fit you anyway since you're such a tiny thing and all he orders is men's size extra large."

"Seriously. I know you've always had a good appetite, Nina, but where are you going to put all of that food?" Barrett didn't hide the fact that his eyes were scanning her from head to toe.

"In my belly." She smiled, not the least bit ashamed.

"Atta, girl." Eileen winked, then moved onto the next table.

Marshall speared a chunk of melon from his bowl. "So back to my question about your parents deciding it was better to skip town than find out the truth."

"You're from the city, right?" Barrett waited for Marshall to nod before continuing. "See, small towns are…different. Sometimes the truth doesn't matter as much as who plays golf with the local judge or what folks are saying about you down at the feed store. College scouts were starting to show interest in me, and all it would've taken was one rumor to end my football career before it started. I guess my parents were just trying to protect me. They knew that if we stayed in Tenacity, my reputation would be stained even if they *could* get the charges dropped."

"Except you didn't end up playing football in college anyway," Nina pointed out. It was starting to look more and more like Barrett's parents had likely overreacted, but that was the luxury of hindsight and not knowing what was going through the Deroys' minds fifteen years ago.

Marshall must've been thinking the same thing because he said, "I'd like to speak to your parents, if I could."

"I can arrange that, but it'll probably need to be over the phone. I seriously doubt they'll come to Tenacity."

"How long are you planning to stay in town?" Marshall asked.

"I guess that depends on how long your grandfather wants to keep an eye on my ranch in Whitehorn. I hired a couple of older teens to handle the day to day feedings and stuff for the summer, but I'll need to go back before school starts up again."

A thrill of excitement rippled through Nina. Barrett didn't commit to an exact departure date, which meant he could potentially be here for the best part of summer. Obviously, it wasn't going to be just like old times. But maybe she could remind him of what he'd been missing since he'd left Tenacity.

Barrett paid the check, even though Nina had eaten most of his waffle. He'd left a big tip for Eileen, who'd been willing to wait on their table after the first server refused. He wasn't here to win anyone over, though. He just wanted to keep a low profile while he cleared his name.

"My office may look like a disaster zone," Marshall said to Barrett and Nina as they walked outside the restaurant. "But at least the Wi-Fi is hooked up so I can begin researching case law. I'd like to start making some inquiries, although I'm not convinced the locals are going to open up to me."

"My uncle Stanley offered to do some investigating," Nina said. "And I'm off the rest of the weekend, so I can ask around and see if Barrett's return to town has jogged anyone's memory."

"Nina, you've already done more than enough," Barrett told her. Besides, he had a feeling that if she kept bringing up his name, the townspeople would think that she was somehow involved. Or worse—that she was considering getting back together with a potential criminal. Not that he had any intention of starting a relationship while everything was still up in the air.

"Barrett," Nina said, his name coming out as a sigh. "I'm not going to argue with you about this."

"Good," he replied, knowing full well that she was about to argue.

"In that case, I'm going to let you two figure out how to go about questioning the locals." Marshall was clearly smart enough to extricate himself from the conversation that surely wouldn't be going Barrett's way. "If you need me, I'll be unpacking boxes over at my office."

When the attorney drove away, Barrett looked at the remaining vehicles in front of the café. He had no idea what Nina drove or really much more than the basics. He was dying to know everything about her, but he also didn't want to give her the wrong idea or mislead her about his intentions.

He cleared his throat. "I left my truck parked at the hotel and walked over."

"Then hop in and I'll drive." Nina held up her keys and

nodded toward an older SUV that was mostly blue, not counting the maroon passenger door and a gray patch where a dent probably used to be in the rear fender.

"Drive where?" Barrett didn't remember agreeing to a destination, let alone going there together.

"I was thinking I'd take you out to Juniper Road, where the missing money was found. I listened to this podcast about how sometimes it's easier to solve a case if you work backward. By now, I'm sure the authorities already did a thorough search, but there could be something around the boulders out there that might trigger a memory or a clue."

Barrett actually had been curious about where the money was found. As far as he knew, there wasn't anything tying him to the location. So maybe if they could prove that some-one else had access to the hiding spot, it would take some of the heat off of him as the prime suspect.

"Fine. But I'll drive."

"I know she looks like she's been through some things, but trust me—Big Betty is as reliable as they come."

"You named your car Big Betty?" His senses were tin-gling, but he wasn't about to mention something that was purely a coincidence.

She pointed at the vanity license plate. "Technically, the previous owner named her that. My cousin Dante has a car dealership in Bronco, and would you believe that some-one just left this beauty stalled in front of the mechanic's bay? Since nobody ever came back to claim it, their loss was my gain."

Barrett recalled tagging along with the Sanchez fam-ily one time for a big Sunday dinner celebration over in Bronco. The details were foggy, but he remembered a cut-throat basketball game in the backyard and the best carne asada he'd ever had. "Your cousin sold you an abandoned car?"

"Of course he didn't sell it to me. He gave it to my brother Luca after overhauling the engine and salvaging the title. Luca had it for a couple of years before passing it on to me. It still runs great."

"I'm sure it does." Barrett tried to keep the skepticism out of his voice. "But don't you think it's a little too... recognizable?"

"That's what I love about it. Everyone knows it's me when I drive by."

"Right. So I don't know if you recall the server inside the café who refused to take our order once I arrived, but it might be better for your reputation if people *don't* notice us driving around town together."

Nina made a dismissive gesture with her hand. "Don't pay any attention to Jocelyn. Last month she didn't want to serve Winona because the sweet old woman made one of her usual psychic predictions. Next week she'll be boycotting a different customer."

"Can't be good for business," Barrett said.

"It's not like there's a ton of restaurant options in Tenacity. Plus, Jocelyn makes these incredible pies that sell out faster than you'd believe. So, the Silver Spur is still able to make a decent profit with her baked goods."

"Sounds like she might've been happier if she'd carried on her parents' bakery." Barrett finally allowed himself to study the empty storefronts along Central Avenue. "Did everything really go this far downhill because of the missing money?"

"It wasn't all because of the money. They called it a renovation fund, but most of it was earmarked for the Tenacity Trail and driving up tourism so the dinosaur-dig

CHRISTY JEFFRIES 45

people would also want to invest here. Business owners were counting on crowded events that would bring in more people. The annual fireworks show was supposed to be our big draw, remember? Even something as simple as a weekly farmers market would have attracted more visitors on a regular basis. But the city can barely afford to maintain the park nowadays." Nina pointed across the street to a concrete slab that used to be the base of a long-gone gazebo. "Volunteers bring their own lawnmowers to keep the grass cut, but the county inspector deemed the playground a safety hazard a couple of years ago and had it hauled away."

Barrett's heart sank when he recognized the empty space where his mom had once pushed him on the swings. "We used to park our bikes over there and use those two trees as the end zone when we played touch football."

"You mean when *you* played touch football." Nina's forehead still crinkled when she pouted. "I always got picked last for the teams, and nobody would ever pass me the ball."

"True," Barrett admitted with a chuckle. "You couldn't catch a football to save your life."

"I made a few catches." Nina jutted her chest forward, drawing his attention to her rounded breasts under her thin T-shirt.

Barrett quickly looked away before his body responded to her. "You did much better as the lookout for the ice-cream truck."

"Remember the ice-cream-truck driver? You guys called him Cheeto, but I don't think that was his real name."

"Of course I remember Cheeto. His truck was always stocked with more chips than ice cream and my mom swore that guy ate more cheese puffs than he sold. He used to let us buy stuff on credit when we didn't bring any money. I'm pretty sure I still have an outstanding balance with him."

"Someone brought up his name as a suspect when the money first went missing," Nina said as she continued walking toward Big Betty. "But nobody had seen him or his truck for at least a month or two before that. I wonder what ever happened to him."

The detour down memory lane was suddenly over, and Barrett was thrust back into the present. "Were there any other suspects besides me and Cheeto?"

"That's what we're about to find out." Nina's statement would've been more motivational if her car key hadn't gotten stuck in the lock. She blew a strand of brown hair out of her face as she twisted and turned the key, but it wouldn't budge. "Don't worry. This happens all the time."

"I'm sure it does. Which is all the more reason for us to take my truck."

"Hold on—I've almost got it," Nina said right before the key broke in half, effectively jamming the lock. She let out a small curse word, then threw up her hands in defeat. "Okay, so I guess you're driving."

Chapter Four

Nina tried not to think about the fact that this was her first time riding alone in a car with Barrett. Her parents hadn't wanted her to go on any official dates until she was sixteen. Probably because they knew that even back then, she and Barrett were physically drawn to each other. They always sat beside each other during carpool, but by the time she became a teen, they were holding hands and soon their relationship had progressed to the kissing stage.

She used to lie awake in her bed at night, envisioning him driving to her house to pick her up for their first real date. He'd come inside and talk to her parents, then he'd open the passenger door for her and their song would already be cued up on the CD player. They'd drive to somewhere fancy and elegant—which meant somewhere outside of Tenacity—and have the most romantic candlelight dinner.

Barrett did open the door for her today, but that was about the only thing that lined up with her schoolgirl fantasy. His truck was new enough that it didn't have a CD player, and she had no idea what kind of music would be on his playlist. There wasn't going to be any candlelight, and their destination was anything but elegant. In fact, now that

Barrett had pulled onto Central Avenue, Nina wondered if it might be best to fill him in on what to expect.

"So are you familiar with Juniper Road?" she asked.

"It's been a while. I think there were a few bigger houses out there. Not that Tenacity ever had what people might consider a wealthier neighborhood, but it wasn't exactly the same part of town of town where we grew up." He slowed at the crosswalk in front of Little Cowpokes Daycare Center, where a dad was running to catch up with a young boy on a bike with training wheels. "Why?"

Nina bit her lower lip. Maybe they should get a bit farther out of town before she told him so that he didn't insist on turning back. "The area where we're going has some uneven terrain. Lots of large rocks and boulders. I just wanted to make sure you were okay with that."

When the crosswalk was clear, Barrett kept his eyes on the road and accelerated. "Is this your polite way of saying I'm not dressed for a hike?"

He was wearing faded jeans and well-worn cowboy boots that had some dust on the heels. The way his white T-shirt stretched over his broad shoulders made Nina's mouth go dry. There wasn't a thing wrong with the way he was dressed except for the fact that he made such a simple clothing choice look so damn good.

"No, you're fine. I mean, what you're wearing is fine." She spotted a pair of sunglasses hooked to his visor and pointed them out. "But it's pretty bright out, so you'll probably want to wear those."

She reached into her tote bag and pulled out her own pair of dark glasses, sliding them onto her face. Looking into the back seat, she saw a tan Stetson and a green ball cap. She unclipped her seat belt, setting off a pinging alarm.

"What are you doing?" he asked.

Stretching to grab the hats off the back seat, she said, "I just thought we should probably wear these, too."

Nina set the Stetson on the console between them and then pulled her hair through the loop in the ball cap before settling it onto her head. She re-buckled her seat belt before nudging the cowboy hat more in his direction.

He made a right onto Juniper Road, then took a second to glance in her direction. She slid the hat over another two inches, and this time, his glance became a much longer look. She wished that he'd put on his sunglasses so that she wouldn't feel the heat of his stare. "Why do you keep looking at me like that?"

"Because I recently found out that you're a successful horse trainer. Which means everything you do is probably for a specific reason, and it's just now popped into my head that there's a chance you're trying to train me."

"I'm not trying to train you, Barrett."

"Good. Because you'll be disappointed to know that I'm not as amenable to leg cues as your former student Bruiser."

"If I give you a leg cue, you'll know it." Nina realized the sexual implication of her words only seconds after she said them and hoped the hat and sunglasses hid the heat spots on her cheeks. "I mean, if I'm trying to get you to do something, then I'll just come out and say it."

"Good to know. Then let's start off with coming out and telling me why you're pushing for both of us to be in disguise while we're driving down this road. Especially after you had no problem driving out here in your very noticeable car."

"When people see my car, they assume I'm on my way to a ranch to see about a horse and don't give me a second glance. Also, my front passenger seat is missing and nobody would've been able to see you sitting in my backseat where the windows are tinted. But your truck is going to draw even more attention to us because people will be wondering who's inside and where we're going." Her shoulders sagged as she exhaled loudly. "It's not a disguise, really. I just think it might be smarter if we're not so recognizable on this side of town."

A car approached from the opposite side of the road, and while Nina resisted the urge to completely duck her head, she did slide a bit lower in the seat.

After it passed, Barrett eased the truck onto the shoulder and came to a complete stop. He reached across the console and gently slid the sunglasses off her face. "What aren't you telling me, Nina?"

"Okay, so I might've forgotten to mention that Darrel Stooler and his wife are the owners of the property. They weren't exactly thrilled to find out that they didn't get to keep the money since it was discovered on their land."

"Was there a dispute about whose money it was?"

"No. The note found with the cash made it pretty clear that it was the missing funds from the town's renovation account."

"Uh-huh." Barrett narrowed his eyes. "What else did the note say?"

"Is my poker face really that bad?" she asked.

"No. But you're forgetting that I could always read you, Nina Sanchez."

A shiver raced up her spine, forcing her to sit upright. He was right, of course. She'd forgotten what it was like to be with the one person who knew her as well as her family did, how thrilling it felt to be so vulnerable and yet so safe at the same time. Could he tell how much she wanted him to kiss her right now?

His nostrils flared slightly, and she realized that he probably could. His voice seemed deeper when he said, "Stop looking at my lips like that and tell me what else the note said."

Apparently, they *weren't* about to kiss.

Nina drew a long breath so she wouldn't sound so disappointed. "It said that the town had the wrong man."

Barrett tilted his head. "Did it mean *I* was the wrong man?"

"That's what I thought it meant at first. But Uncle Stanley pointed out that you were technically still a boy at the time. So maybe they meant another man? A grown man. Of course, if the person who hid the money was the same person who stole it, then why leave a note at all?"

"Maybe the person who wrote the note wasn't the thief but knows who was," Barrett suggested. "Maybe they followed the thief to the hiding spot and put the note there after the fact?"

"But wouldn't it have made more sense to simply tell the authorities where the money was?"

"Not if they were trying to protect whoever stole it," he said, and Nina thought about that possibility. "You're trying to imagine if you would have done the same thing if you'd known that I was the thief."

"Stop trying to read me, Barrett. But yes, that's exactly what I was imagining. And the answer is that I *wouldn't* have done the same thing. I'm sorry to say that I wouldn't have kept that big of a secret. Even if it meant protecting you."

"I know. Which is one of the things I loved about you back then. Your sense of justice and needing to do the right thing."

What he'd loved about her *back then*. Past tense. She couldn't allow herself to overthink his words. They were both adults now. Of course they weren't going to feel the same way they'd felt when they were teenagers. It wasn't like she still loved him, either. Or at least this version of him. She didn't even know who he was anymore.

Which was why she didn't want him to keep reading her expressions, why she didn't want him thinking he knew her better than she knew him.

Nina cleared her throat and took the sunglasses out of his hand, ignoring the way her fingers accidentally brushed his. "Anyway, the Stoolers didn't want to deal with all the speculation that came along with the money being found on their land, so they had the sheriff's office put up some of that yellow tape."

"You mean the kind that says 'Police Line, Do Not Cross'?"

She waved her hand dismissively. "Who knows what exactly it says on it? I haven't been there since the initial discovery. For all I know, it could say something about watching for falling rocks. It really is uneven terrain. You'll see when we get there."

"Nina." His warning tone reminded her of her father's whenever Will Sanchez was about to drive his wife to the fabric store for material he didn't think she needed. "I'm already a person of interest in this case. I don't need to add trespassing, let alone interfering with an active investigation, to my list of potential crimes."

"I thought Marshall confirmed that you might not be a person of interest anymore. At least not formally."

"If you really believed that, then you wouldn't be making us wear disguises when we get there."

"Really, Barrett? The word *disguises* is a bit dramatic. We're just wearing hats and glasses. The same things we would be wearing if we were driving around anywhere else in town. Speaking of which, you should put yours on before another car comes by." When he only stared at her and made no move to follow her advice, she picked up the Stetson and plopped it onto his head. "We already look pretty suspicious pulled off the road like this."

Barrett groaned as he adjusted the brim. "Does anyone ever tell you no, Nina?"

"Sometimes," she said, then gulped when she saw how incredibly hot the man looked in a cowboy hat.

"Who? Because I really want to meet the person who can put the determined Miss Sanchez in her place."

"I didn't say I let anyone put me in my place. All I said is that people sometimes try to tell me no."

"Try?" he asked.

She smiled. "Usually it's someone who doesn't know me."

Nina Sanchez was going to be the death of him.

Barrett shook his head as he followed the slender but shapely woman as she easily hopped from one large rock onto the next, her dark brown ponytail swinging under the green ball cap she'd snatched from his back seat.

"It's just over here," Nina called out as she jumped to a small clearing of grass that was matted down by mud and at least half a dozen tire tracks. Several flimsy stakes held scraps of torn yellow caution tape that flapped in the warm breeze. Half of a torn sign that might've once said "NO TRESPASSING" was nailed to a tree, the remaining letters reading O PASSING.

"Tell me again why we couldn't have just driven up here like everyone else in town has apparently done?" Barrett used the toe of his boot to kick aside a wadded up fast-food bag and a broken bottle. "Looks like someone hosted quite the party."

"It's summer break and most of the kids in Tenacity grew up hearing stories about the mystery of the missing town funds. You know how teenagers can be."

Barrett actually had limited knowledge of how they could be. He'd been too busy playing sports and keeping his grades up to attend field parties. Then he'd been forced to spend the last years of his adolescence on the run. But he didn't need Nina feeling sorry for him.

"Well, at least we don't have to worry about contaminating a crime scene. It's already been pretty well trampled on."

"So this is it." Nina pointed to an area covered with so many excavated holes, it was one rainstorm away from becoming a mudslide. "It looks like there might've been a few treasure hunters who stopped by to see if there was any more money hidden out here."

Barrett knelt near one of the deeper trenches. "Was the money buried inside anything? Like a bag or a container of some sort?"

"Actually, it was stashed inside a fake boulder. You know, one of those big plastic things you can buy at a garden store that are hollow inside?"

Barrett nodded. "So the cash was just sitting there all loose?"

"Yep. Just rolled up with a folded note."

Barrett lifted his head and surveyed the land around him. "Didn't the fake boulder stand out compared to all the real ones out here?"

"Not after fifteen years of weather beating down on it. Besides, it's private property, so it's not like anyone off the street would come walking through this area."

"Wait. Didn't the Woodsons used to live out on Juniper Road?"

Nina's adorable nose scrunched beneath the frames of her dark glasses. "So that's the other thing I probably should have told you before we came out here. Before the Stoolers bought it, this property used to belong to the Woodsons."

Barrett's blood went cold, which was difficult to do on a warm summer day. "As in Brent Woodson, the guy who benefitted the most by me leaving town?"

"Yes, but did I mention that they haven't lived here in years?"

Barrett ignored Nina's attempt to appease him. "As in Mayor Woodson who drove out to my house in the middle of the night to accuse me of being a thief? You're telling me the missing money was on their property this whole time?"

"Well, it was on their property until they sold the land."

"And nobody thought it was strange that they didn't take the money with them when they moved?"

"As a matter of fact, several people thought it was strange. Which only went to prove that the Woodsons couldn't possibly be the ones who hid the money here."

"I think it proves the opposite. But what do I know? I'm simply the poor kid who was blamed for the crime and had to leave his home in the dead of night and live with a secret identity for the past fifteen years." Barrett clasped his hands behind his neck, looking up at the sky and stretching the tension out of his muscles as he made a full circle turn. "Why is this town so damn backward? How was it so easy for them to blame me for something that was hiding behind a stupid fake rock all this time? Or better yet, why didn't anyone do an actual investigation and try to find the missing money? Instead, everyone just pointed the finger at some helpless sixteen-year-old and then sat around while the playground at the park fell apart and stores went out of business and the entire economic backbone of the town went under."

His angry outburst could've caused a timid woman to recoil from him in caution. Yet he felt the weight of Nina's gaze as she openly studied him. He barely heard her soft-spoken words when she said, "Not everyone."

"What?"

She took a step closer to him. "Not everyone pointed the finger at you, Barrett. Some of us have been doing every-thing we could to prove that you weren't the one to blame."

"I know," he sighed, dropping his arms to his sides.

"No, Barrett, I don't think you do know. I'm not saying that I suffered as much as you did back then. But my world was still turned upside down. I didn't go to prom because I'd heard a rumor that someone's aunt's friend spotted you at a seafood restaurant in Bozeman. My mom had sewn me this gorgeous dress, and instead of putting it on and taking photos and dancing the night away with my friends who were about to leave for college, I borrowed Diego's old truck and drove hundreds of miles to Anchors Ahoy, where it was all-you-can-eat shrimp night. And guess what?"

"You didn't find me working at the Anchors Ahoy," he answered.

"Correct. You also weren't working at the Crab Palace or the Lobster House or even the Long John Silver's."

"I didn't know there were that many all-you-can-eat shrimp restaurants in a state where beef is king."

"And I went to them all. Every time there was a possible lead about where you might be, I would drop everything and head out on a wild-goose chase. Only to have my hopes crushed time and time again. Did you know I got offered a full-ride scholarship to Texas A&M?"

His eyes snapped up. "That was your dream school."

"I know. I didn't go because I convinced myself that you'd be coming back to Tenacity any day and I didn't want to be living out of state when that happened."

"Nina, you shouldn't have put your dreams on hold for me."

"No, I shouldn't have. But I believed with all my heart that I could somehow find you, that I could prove your innocence. So don't tell me that everyone just sat around and let this happen. It might've taken me fifteen years, but you being here today is because *I* didn't give up." She pointed a finger at her own chest. "Because *I* didn't take no for an answer."

Aw, hell. He had never wanted to haul someone into his arms and kiss them more than he did at that exact second. He'd also never felt more unworthy of someone's loyalty. Barrett should have reached out to her back then. He should have been as determined as she'd been all those years ago. Sure, he'd naively thought he was protecting her reputation, that by staying away, he was allowing her to move on with her life. But maybe he was also protecting himself from the reality of having to face the fact that her life was better without him.

"You're right," he admitted. "You never gave up on me. I should've had more faith in you. At minimum, I should have called to check in on you. I definitely should have talked you out of your asinine plan to throw away a scholarship to Texas."

"Don't worry. My dad didn't let me throw it away completely." She adjusted the hat on her head. "The school let me take some online courses at first, and when I realized that you could find me if you really wanted to, I did move out there to finish my last two years. But I didn't attend a single football game because it reminded me too much of you. And I came back to Montana as soon as I graduated."

Still. Neither of them had gotten to have the full college experience they'd once envisioned for themselves. She'd already given up so much for him, even if he hadn't asked her to. No matter how powerful his attraction still was for her, he wasn't going to subject her to any more strife. Not while his future was up in the air and certainly not while she thought they needed disguises just to drive through town. And saying goodbye to Nina a second time was something he couldn't bear to do.

Which meant Barrett had to keep his hands to himself. As physically painful as it was to not hold her right now, to not comfort her and tell her that everything was going to be all right, he knew that he would only be making it worse if he gave either of them false hope.

Instead, he focused on what he'd come here to focus on.

"So where's the money now?"

Chapter Five

It was easy for Nina to conclude that Barrett no longer felt the same way about her. After all, she'd practically poured her heart out to him a few minutes ago and he hadn't bothered to offer her so much as a comforting hug. In fact, in the past twenty-four hours, he seemed to shy away from any sort of physical contact with her.

Last night, she could understand that tensions were high and emotions were raw, especially after he'd almost gotten into a fistfight with Brent Woodson. Even this morning, though, when they sat beside each other at breakfast, Barrett kept as much distance as possible between them. Any touch had seemed accidental and was way too brief.

It wasn't like she was throwing herself at the man, but did he now have to act as though he was one of her big brothers? She already had three of those and didn't need a fourth.

Leaving the Stooler property, Barrett had again opened the truck door for her. But he was the type of guy who would do that for any woman he was with. For a split second, Nina wondered if it would've been easier if he hadn't come back. If she wasn't better off holding on to the young, happier version of Barrett who lived in her memories.

No. That wasn't fair. She shook off the thought as quickly

as it had popped into her mind. Nina wasn't the same person anymore either. She couldn't expect them to just pick up where they'd once left off. Nor should she want them to. They'd both grown into different people with their own different lives.

Still. As she stared out the truck window, she wished there was something she could say to end this awkward silence between them. Nina ached to have Barrett hold her the way he used to. But she ached even more for his friendship. When they were young, everything had been so effortless. They went together like peanut butter and jelly. Right now, though, things felt like oil and water. And sweat. Man, it was getting hot in this truck.

She rolled down the window and tossed the ball cap she'd been wearing into the back seat, letting the wind whip through her hair.

"You aren't afraid someone might see you riding around town with me?" Barrett asked.

"Now that we left Juniper Road? Not in the slightest." As if to prove it, she propped her elbow in the open windowsill and turned her face toward the fresh air coming from outside. As they passed the next house, she saw Mrs. Ferguson out watering her lawn and waved.

"She didn't wave back," Barrett pointed out.

"We were driving by so fast, she probably just didn't recognize me."

Barrett checked his rearview mirror. "Judging by the finger she's holding up, I'm pretty sure she recognized who was in the driver's seat."

"I told you before that not everyone in town feels that way, Barrett. Besides, Mrs. Ferguson has always been an old grouch. My dad said she once flipped off Mayor Woodson at a city council meeting when they passed a water-rate hike to help offset the town's budget deficit."

"Remember that time we played our homecoming game against Bronco High?" Barrett chuckled. "Mrs. Ferguson gave their whole team the middle finger when they were running onto the field, and Coach Parker had to tell her that if she didn't knock it off, the refs would kick her out of the game."

Nina practically snorted at the memory, and suddenly they were both giggling like a couple of little kids. It felt so good to finally laugh together. This was how things were supposed to be between them. She needed to figure out a way to keep this mood up.

Maybe going someplace familiar might spark another funny memory. Or at least remind Barrett of how things used to be.

Nina knew just the spot.

"You know what I could go for right now?" Nina said when Barrett pulled onto Central Avenue. "A basket of fries and a milkshake at the Tenacity Social Club."

"Seriously?" Barrett's hat had joined the other one in the back seat, and the wind was ruffling the longish strands of his wavy brown hair. "I can't believe that old speakeasy is still around."

Technically, the Tenacity Social Club hadn't been a speakeasy since Prohibition ended almost a hundred years ago. It had originally been built to be a simple bar, and it still served alcohol. But over the years it had evolved into a gathering place for the young and the old to hang out, listen to music, and commiserate about everything from algebra homework to divorce settlements. It was also where people would go to celebrate a job promotion or a winning baseball game. But it was the perfect place to go when you didn't want to feel alone.

"Hardly anything has changed. You've got to see it to believe it," Nina challenged. "It's only four thirty on a Saturday. We can go now before it gets busy."

"Fine. But if it starts filling up with townspeople carrying pitchforks and wearing T-shirts that say 'I hate Barrett Deroy,' then you'll need to sneak me out the back door."

"I promise," Nina told him with a straight face, knowing full well that there actually was a time when someone suggested the town make money by selling T-shirts with a similar slogan. To her knowledge, nobody ever had them made. But there had been a few handwritten yard signs back in the day. "You can even park in the alley behind the post office if it makes you feel better."

She tried to make her tone sound as playful as possible, but mentally, she sent up a silent prayer that they wouldn't really need to utilize any sort of escape plan. Her confidence must've been contagious because Barrett did the opposite of her suggestion and parked on the street right in front of the stairs leading down to the Tenacity Social Club's entrance.

"Bold move." She smiled. "I like it that you're feeling more comfortable in town."

"Actually, I figured that by now, most people will know what I'm driving. I'd prefer not to give anyone the opportunity to bust out my windshield or spray paint something unflattering on the side of my truck. At least not out in the open and during the light of day."

"Also a bold move," Nina said, then quickly let herself out of the vehicle before Barrett changed his mind.

Barrett opened the heavy oak door and immediately saw that Nina had once again been right. Not much inside the Tenacity Social Club had changed. The jukebox was still in the corner. The small stage was currently empty, but judging by the flyers stuck to the bulletin board near the entrance, a band he'd never heard of would be performing on it later tonight. Even the old pinball machine was the same, although its neon-lit screen now boasted a higher score than Barrett had once held the record to.

He recognized Josh Aventura, who'd been a few years ahead of Barrett in school, sitting at the opposite end of the long wooden bar with a well-dressed brunette who looked vaguely familiar. The couple was in deep conversation with Shane Corey and his grandparents. There were a couple of other customers, but like Nina had predicted, the place wasn't busy at all. At least not yet. She pulled out a barstool, and it didn't take Barrett long to remember that this was the exact spot where they used to sit when they'd come here after school.

The only noticeable change was the bartender who was walking toward them. The man looked to be around the same age as them, but Barrett didn't recognize him. He smiled as he put a couple of napkins in front of them and said, "Hey, Nina. What can I get you two?"

"Well, before I walked in, I had my heart set on some fries and a milkshake." Nina glanced at her watch. "But now that I see Amy's queso and chips, I think I want some of those. And maybe a margarita."

Amy Hawkins. That was why the brunette at the end of the bar looked so familiar. But what was a famous rodeo star doing in Tenacity? Before Barrett could ask that very question, Nina was introducing him to the bartender. "Barrett, do you remember Mike Cooper? He and his twin sister were a couple of years behind me in school."

"I remember the Cooper Ranch." Barrett reached across the bar top to shake the man's hand.

"So the famous Barrett Deroy finally returns." Mike's friendly smile—and the use of the word *famous* instead of *infamous*—possibly proved Nina's earlier assertion that not everyone in town hated the Deroys. "More pieces of the puzzle are coming together."

"Mike's the one who helped me ask around about Juniper Road," Nina added. "Which led to us finding the missing money, which led to you finally coming back to town."

"So I take it Nina enlisted you in her grand plan to lay the groundwork for my redemption tour?"

"Redemption Tour sounds like the name of one of the bands scheduled to play here later this summer." Mike nodded toward Otis Corey, the older man at the other side of the bar. "Besides, I'm not sure how much redemption you're going to need with Mr. Corey over there reminding everyone else in town who still holds the record for most touchdown passes at Tenacity High."

"He's talking about you, in case you forgot." Nina patted Barrett's back, then left her hand there. It felt warm and comforting, and he wouldn't be opposed to it sliding lower toward his waist. "Mike's best friend, Jenna, is engaged to my brother Diego. He's also the godfather to her daughter and my soon-to-be niece, Robbie."

"Which reminds me." Mike flipped a bar towel over his shoulder. "I need to talk to Jenna about the seating arrangements at the wedding. Danny is coming as my plus one and we're going to want to avoid another conversation about his precious Bronco High School once losing to Tenacity High in the quarterfinals to State."

"Mike's boyfriend Daniel is one of…" Nina lowered her voice to a whisper and used finger quotes "…'those Taylors' from Bronco."

Mike laughed at Nina's dramatic description of one of

the wealthiest families in Montana. "Last time I checked, you have a Sanchez cousin that's married to one of those Taylors. And your sister, Marisa, didn't have a problem marrying into a wealthy Bronco family either."

The rivalry between Tenacity High and Bronco High was legendary enough in this part of Montana. But there was a secondary social distinction when it came to the city over an hour away from here, and everyone knew there was a difference between being from the affluent Bronco Heights and living in the more blue-collar Bronco Valley.

Barrett lifted an eyebrow at Nina. "You said Marisa moved to Bronco. You didn't tell me she was living in the Heights."

"What can I say?" Nina's hand eased down to Barrett's lower back. "We Sanchez women have great taste in men."

"I'd say 'Cheers' to that," Mike offered. "But I'm working and you two don't have your drinks yet."

"I'll take an IPA," Barrett said quickly. He needed something to cool his blood down before Nina's hand made any further movements. "Whatever you have on tap that's cold."

A Brooks & Dunn song came on the jukebox and a chorus of yeehaws sounded from a table in the corner.

"I know what you're going to ask, Barrett." Nina's hand dropped away from his back and she reached into her purse and pulled out a single bill. "And the answer is yes, you can still select four songs for a dollar."

"Looks like Mrs. Corey beat us to it. I just saw her put a ten into the jukebox." Which explained why Mr. Corey wouldn't be coming over to this side of the bar any time soon to talk football. His wife was leading him toward an open area to do the boot scootin' boogie.

Mike returned with two frosty mugs—one filled with

beer and one filled with something even colder and a rim covered in salt. Barrett paused as he stared at their drinks.

"You did say an IPA, right?" Mike asked.

"Yeah. Sorry." Barrett picked up his glass. "It's just that I don't think I ever drank anything stronger than a Shirley Temple in this place."

"Barrett and I used to come here when we were kids," Nina explained to the bartender. "In fact, these are our initials right here."

When Barrett saw Nina's finger trace the lopsided heart carved into the wooden bar, his own heart began to beat faster. He couldn't stop his finger from reaching out to follow the same path hers had just taken.

When he lifted his gaze, he found her studying him intently. Not breaking eye contact, she took a long sip of her margarita.

"Are we having another staring contest?" he asked, taking an even longer drink of his own beer.

She lowered her glass. "No. I was just waiting for you to remember something."

"What's that?" His voice sounded raspy, like he'd swallowed too much foam. But he knew that wasn't the cause. He was well on his way to being aroused by the most beautiful woman in this place. In this entire state.

"Do you remember what you said to me the day you carved that?"

He didn't bother pretending that he didn't know what she was talking about. "I said that we were now an official part of Tenacity's history. That anyone who ever stepped foot in this club would know about our love."

It had probably seemed corny coming from an inexperienced kid, but Barrett remembered firmly believing that he and Nina were destined to be a grand love story for the ages.

Her drink was halfway gone when she asked, "Do you think it would've lasted?"

"What?"

She playfully shoved his arm. "Us. Do you think if you would have stayed through high school, we could have lasted?"

If she kept touching him like this, he wasn't sure he'd be able to last the night without pulling her into his arms. That wasn't what she meant, though. Again, he answered honestly.

"I don't know." He downed more beer. "It's a dangerous game, playing *what if*. What if I stayed? What if you met someone you liked better than me in high school?"

"Who would I have possibly liked better than you?" she asked.

"Brent?"

"As if." She was keeping up with him, sip for sip. "What if you went off to college and met some hot premed student who was wealthy and glamorous and wanted to have a dozen of your children?"

"You didn't want to have a dozen of my children?" He finished his beer.

"No way." She signaled Mike for another round. "Remember my vow about never driving a minivan after I got carsick in the back of my mom's? I'm good for maybe two kids—three max."

This was the exact reason why Barrett knew not to play the *what-if* game. Now he was sitting here, watching another couple now dancing next to the Coreys, thinking about what his and Nina's two kids—three max—would be like.

A wooden platter holding a small iron skillet arrived, and Nina used a chip to dip into the hot, spicy cheese dip with the same enthusiasm she'd had earlier at the Silver Spur. Although she did keep the plate between them so they could share.

Barrett took a couple of chips and decided to throw her a more challenging question. "What if I didn't go off to college?"

"Oh come on, Barrett. You had scouts coming to games your freshman year. There was no way you weren't going to get a scholarship."

"What if I broke my arm?"

"Then you'd get a cast and be better the following season."

"What if it was a career-ending injury?"

She picked up her fresh drink from the second round Mike had just set in front of them. "Like your arm got stuck in a woodchipper?"

Barrett choked on his beer. "Okay, you apparently still watch way too many crime documentaries."

"That was actually in a show about true stories from emergency rooms. Wood-chipper injuries are more common than you'd think. But fine. What if you had a career-ending, non-wood-chipper-related injury and couldn't go to college?"

"I mean, I kind of had a career-ending criminal accusation and a life on the run. That didn't stop me from going to college. Just like having an ex-boyfriend on the lam didn't stop you from going to college. We both found a way."

"I guess what I'm asking is what if something happened and we both ended up staying in Tenacity? Both of us working local jobs and coming here to the Social Club every Saturday. Do you think we would've lasted? That we would've been as happy as we thought we'd be?"

"I don't know. I guess so."

"Because statistically speaking, marrying your high school sweetheart doesn't always work out."

"Statistically speaking, my arm isn't going to get stuck in a wood chipper either." Man, this second round was going down even faster than the first. "Wait. Are you saying that you think we would have eventually broken up anyway?"

"Anyway?" she asked. "Technically, we never broke up the first time around."

"Nina, we haven't seen each other for fifteen years. I'm pretty sure that's considered a breakup."

She wiggled her eyebrows playfully. "Yeah, but neither one of us ever said the official words to end things."

Nina had always enjoyed challenging him, but Barrett was no longer sure they were only teasing. He set down his beer. "Are you saying that we're still boyfriend and girlfriend?"

The jukebox switched over to a pop song. "If we were, then you would know what happens every time this song comes on."

OutKast began the first line and Barrett chuckled when he recognized "Hey Ya!" "I am not dancing with you, Nina Sanchez."

"Come on, Barrett. I taught you the steps myself. We performed our routine for the entire middle school."

"No, *you* performed it for the entire middle school. Luca and I just hung out behind you and pretended to play the drums and keyboard."

Nina laughed. "You guys were the worst backup dancers ever. I think my mom still has the video at home."

They talked about some of their more awkward adolescent moments and laughed over shared stories about different teachers and classmates.

Barrett realized time had flown by as they'd reminisced

and the Social Club was filling up with more people. A band was setting up on the small stage, even though the jukebox was still going strong.

"It's getting late." He signaled to Mike for the check. "I should probably get back to my room."

"You paid for our meal earlier today." Nina reached into her purse. "Coming here was my idea, so I should pay."

"That's not how this works," Barrett said as he gave the bartender cash. "Besides, I'm pretty sure tagging along for my meeting with the attorney at the Silver Spur was also your idea."

A slow song came on, and a few more people went to the area in front of the stage that now served as the dance floor.

"In that case—" Nina grinned "—I have one more idea."

"Should I even ask?" Barrett could only imagine what Nina had thought up. "I doubt you'd let me tell you no anyway."

"Then don't bother telling me no now." When she stood up and grabbed his hand, her intentions became just as clear as his empty beer glass.

Nope. This wasn't going to happen. He stayed planted on his seat, shaking his head from side to side.

"Oh, come on, Barrett." Her pink lips pushed forward. "I haven't even asked yet."

"I already know what you're going to ask."

"Then I'm not asking." The pout had turned into a playful grin. "Dance with me, Barrett."

He shook his head again, but he was pivoted enough on his stool that she was able to stand between his open legs.

"Then I'll just put my arms around you like this." She slid her palms behind his neck, and he nearly groaned. But not out of frustration.

"And I'll start swaying like this." She moved her hips

slowly from side to side, and Barrett felt his jeans grow tighter.

"Oh, look," she whispered into his ear. "We're dancing."

"The hell we are," he growled as put his arm around her waist and got to his feet. He had her pulled so tight against his body, he was practically carrying her as he walked her backward toward the unofficial dance floor. "If we're going to do this, Nina, we're going to do it right."

Chapter Six

Barrett had known that the moment he took Nina into his arms, he might not be able to let her go again. Man, he had never wanted to be more wrong in his life. Unfortunately, as she swayed her body against his, moving to the slow rhythm, he realized that he had never been more right.

They fit together even better than before. His face was tilted toward her loose, dark hair, and he inhaled deeply, letting the familiar scent of jasmine further intoxicate him. Her rounded breasts pressed against the thin fabric of his T-shirt, and Barrett immediately knew that her body was just as affected as his was. She tightened her arms around his neck, which caused the hem of her shirt to rise higher, exposing a strip of silky soft skin under his pinky fingers. Thankfully, the music was loud enough to cover his groan as he let his hands flirt with the warm promise of what would happen if he allowed them to slip underneath the cotton fabric.

He felt Nina's soft breath above the collar of his shirt and wondered if she could see his pulse jumping against the skin of his neck. Barrett didn't dare pull his head back to look at her, because he didn't trust himself not to get so distracted that he ran into another couple on the dance floor.

And that was when he remembered that he and Nina

weren't the only people in the place. Although he was pretty sure they were the only ones who had an audience. Several people at the bar were looking over their shoulders, and Barrett made a slight pivot to steer Nina away from the curious eyes. But as he turned, he noticed someone standing next to the jukebox, scowling in their direction.

Uh-oh.

Barrett instinctively took a step back, putting some distance between him and Nina, and she suddenly opened her eyes, which were either glazed with passion or the effects of her two margaritas.

"Don't look now," he whispered, "but someone is watching us, and he looks pretty pissed."

She blinked twice, then did the exact opposite of Barrett's directions by fully pivoting to face her brother.

The timing couldn't have been any worse because Keith Urban chose that exact moment to end the song. Which meant everyone was able to hear Nina say, "What are you doing here, Luca?"

Except her brother didn't bother to acknowledge her, let alone answer the question. His attention was focused solely on Barrett. "You back to break her heart again, Deroy?"

Wow. His former friend's accusation was a sucker punch compared to Brent Woodson's drunk allegation last night. It wasn't like Barrett expected the rest of the Sanchez family to welcome him as kindly as Nina had. But he also hadn't expected such hostility from the man he'd once considered to be the closest thing he had to a brother.

"That is the last thing I want to do." Barrett returned Luca's appraising glare. "In fact, I wasn't trying to break it fifteen years ago, either."

Luca, who'd always been the quietest Sanchez brother, must've realized that they now had the attention of everyone inside the Tenacity Social Club. He took a step closer and lowered his voice. "Except you did. And I was left picking up the pieces."

"The pieces?" Nina rolled her eyes at her brother. "Luca, you make it sound like I was a fragile vase shattered against the wall. I was upset. Yes, I was even brokenhearted. But don't act like you weren't just as devastated as me."

"Of course I was devastated, Nina." Luca was finally addressing his sister, but he was still looking straight at Barrett. "You might've lost your boyfriend, but I lost my best friend. And yes, Barrett was *my* friend first. Long before you two became a couple."

Okay. So that was what this was about. Barrett released a long breath, along with some of the tension coiled in his muscles. "You're right, Luca. I owe you just as much of an explanation as I owed Nina. And if you let me buy you a beer, I'll give you one."

"You owe me a helluva lot more than a beer and an explanation, Deroy. But I don't think you're going to have time for that."

"Actually, Luca, Barrett is planning stay in Tenacity for a while," Nina said. "So there's plenty of time for you two to talk things out and—"

"That's not what he means, Nina," Barrett interrupted at the exact same time Luca said, "That's not what I mean, Nina."

"Yep, I still hate it when you two do that weird best-friend-telepathy thing you do where you both talk over me."

Barrett felt her staring at him, but he was busy staring at Luca, waiting for the man to explain his warning. Because he might not have seen it in a long time, but he still knew that look in his friend's eyes.

"Brent and a couple of his buddies are over at the Grizzly

right now watching the last inning of the Rockies game and finishing their third pitcher of beer. But as soon as that's over, they plan on finding you so they can have a friendly little chat to resolve some unfinished business." Luca's sarcastic tone indicated just what kind of "chat" Brent Woodson intended to have. And that it was going to be anything but friendly.

Barrett flexed his fingers, wondering how many punches he could get in before the golden boy of Tenacity commanded his little followers to jump in and make it an unfair fight.

Luca nodded toward Barrett's clenched fists. "Listen, man. Brent isn't the pompous jerk he used to be in high school. But he's had a lot to drink this weekend and a lot of people chirping in his ear about you. So if you want to avoid causing an even bigger scene than the one you just made on the dance floor, I'd suggest you get my sister out of here."

"I can get myself out of here." Nina's puffed out chest would've conveyed a tougher image if she didn't have that adorable blush on her cheeks.

"No, you can't." Her brother pulled a detached door handle out of his back pocket. "Big Betty's locking mechanism is officially shot, and Dad is gonna have a fit if you ask him for one more bungie cord, roll of duct tape, or piece of rope to hold that thing together."

"Come on." Barrett dropped an arm around Nina's shoulders. "I'll give you a ride home."

It was that second that Barrett realized he might be walking into a more hostile environment with even more Sanchezes shooting daggers at him the way Luca had a few moments ago.

"I'll let Mom and Dad know you're leaving now." Luca already had his phone out, and his thumbs were flying across the screen. He shoved it back into his pocket. "So be sure you don't take any detours on the way."

Like waving a red cape in front of a bull, Luca had practically just dared his sister to do the exact opposite. Barrett shot his former friend a look of disbelief.

"In case you didn't get the memo, Luca, I'm a grown woman." Nina exhaled loudly—and rather dramatically—and walked back toward their barstools. Barrett and Luca were both left to follow her. She pulled her own phone out of her purse and began tapping. Then she slung her bag over her shoulder and said, "I told Mom and Dad not to wait up."

Barrett tightened his jaw, determined not to let her recklessness override his good sense. He didn't care how grown Nina thought she was. He was taking her straight home.

"I know what you're thinking, Barrett Deroy," Nina said when they pulled away from the curb just as the sun was going down.

"What am I thinking?" He sped up as he headed toward the side of town where he and Nina were raised.

"That you can drop me off and pretend that what happened back there on the dance floor didn't mean anything."

"Actually, hearing Luca admit that he was pissed at me for leaving was a pretty big deal." Barrett dipped his chin. "It did mean something because we really were best friends back in the day. I missed him almost as much as I missed you. I'm not expecting him to forgive me anytime soon, but at least he still cares about me enough to warn me about Brent."

"Yeah, that was a big deal and the last thing I expected Luca to admit." She crossed her arms over her seat-belt strap, determined not to let him change the subject. "But you know that wasn't what I was talking about. So don't make me say it."

"I'm not going to pretend that things didn't get a little out of control on the dance floor. I'm not proud of making it a public display, but yes, it meant something. It also felt damn good to know that we're no longer teenagers and no-body can tell us what we should and shouldn't be doing."

Nina's heart stalled, then started again, thumping hard behind her rib cage. "Good. Because I have no intention of going home tonight."

Barrett's fingers flexed against the steering wheel as he gripped it tighter. His voice was husky when he asked, "So then where do you want me to drop you off?"

"Make your next right."

He slowed and saw the lit sign by the road. The Tenac-ity Inn. "Nina, you know you can't come back to my room with me."

"No, I don't know that all. You just said yourself that we're not kids anymore, Barrett. If I want to spend the night with you, then that's what I'm going to do."

"What if I don't want company?" His voice was low and raw and left no doubt in Nina's mind that he wanted her as much as she wanted him.

But she wasn't going to beg. "Then you better make it very clear right now."

He cursed, then sped up as he passed the driveway. Nina squeezed her eyes shut as if she could hold back her dis-appointment. When she opened them again a few seconds later, she was surprised to see him pulling into the nar-row, unlit service entrance behind the inn. "I scoped out the parking back here last night, out of habit."

He didn't have to explain his thought process. She imag-ined that his parents had taught him all about keeping a low profile and knowing where the rear exits were in case someone—like the cops—came looking for you.

"We'll still need to walk in through the front because guest keycards don't work on the employee entrance. But my truck will draw less attention back here."

Barrett barely had the vehicle in Park when Nina unclipped her seat belt and all but threw herself over the center console and into his arms. He responded by using one hand to anchor her hip and the other to pull her face closer to his so that his lips could claim hers.

His kiss was even better than she'd remembered, more mature and more intense. Her mouth opened expectantly as his tongue explored. Shifting her knee across his lap, she planted herself firmly against him, moaning deeply as the passion exploded between them.

Nina had no idea how long they made out in the close quarters of his driver's seat, but when Barrett's hands moved under her shirt, she threw back her head, pressing her aching breasts toward him. Someone's elbow—possibly hers—bumped the steering wheel, and a startling blast of the truck's horn reminded Nina of where they were.

"We should go inside," she whispered as he trailed kisses along her jaw.

"Except I don't have any protection."

She glanced at her watch. "I'm pretty sure Tenacity Drugs & Sundries is closed by now. There's the gas station down the street, but there's no telling who'd we run into at the quick mart. It's already been fifteen years, and I really don't want to wait any longer."

"Nina," Barrett groaned, his head falling against the leather headrest. Nina used the opportunity to press her lips to the spot on his neck that she'd been desperate to kiss while they'd been dancing. "I can't risk it."

"Risk what?" It wasn't like she was purposely trying to grind against him, but her core instinctively craved more contact with him.

This time, his groan sounded more like a moan. His breathing was ragged as he spoke. "I've always been super cautious about bringing a child into the world when all I can offer that kid is a fake name and a hidden identity."

Nina wanted to tell him that he had so much more to offer a child than that. But she wasn't exactly in a hurry to become a mom, either. At least not yet. She wanted tonight to only be about them. Her breath was equally strained as she spoke between kisses. "It's not like...we have to...you know." She made a whimpering sound when Barrett licked her lower lip. "We can...still do...other things."

"Fine. For now." Barrett opened the driver's-side door, holding Nina against him so tightly, she had no choice but to keep her legs wrapped around his waist as he climbed down. "But I'm buying condoms as soon as the drugstore opens tomorrow."

Nina was counting on it. They weren't even inside the hotel yet, and she already knew how good it was going to be between them. Judging by the way his body responded to hers, Barrett knew it as well.

He kissed her long and deep, and by the time her feet were on the asphalt, she doubted she could stand up on her own. A door under a sign that read Deliveries opened, and a teen who looked vaguely familiar to Nina propped it open with a chair.

"Come on," Barrett whispered. "Let's see if we can go in this way."

He showed his key card to the high school–aged boy who was clearly more concerned about inserting a cartridge into his vape pen than questioning why hotel guests would be using the employee entrance. Nina held on to Barrett's hand as he led her past a short corridor and a linen supply room before going through a door that led to the main hallway on the first floor.

They resumed making out when they got into the elevator, and when it dinged open, Nina let out a tiny squeak when she saw a person wearing a name tag and carrying a stack of towels. Now probably wasn't the time to tell him that her brother Julian's fiancée, Ruby, worked at the inn. Nina didn't think the night shift employee saw her, so hopefully, they wouldn't be able to pass along the info that Nina was sneaking into Barrett's room.

Apparently, the walk from the elevator to Barrett's room was long enough to cool some of his passion because when they finally got inside, he turned toward her, his expression very serious.

"I should probably tell you that it's not just about kids and a lack of condoms," Barrett said.

"What do you mean?"

"The reason why we should be cautious. Just because I can't think straight when you're this close to me doesn't mean I'm ready for *anything* more serious than this. I need my life to be settled before I can pursue any sort of romantic relationship." He somehow managed to keep his hands to himself throughout his little speech, despite the fact that she could tell it was taking every ounce of self-control he had. "I think it's only fair for you to know that before things go any further."

"Nobody is asking for forever, Barrett." She slid her arms back up to his shoulders. "For all we know, it might end up being awful between us."

That was the last thing Nina remembered saying before Barrett proceeded to prove her wrong.

"Nina?" Barrett whispered into her ear as she was dozing off.

"Hmmm…?" She nestled herself against him. They were still partially clothed, lying on top of the covers after using their mouths and hands to bring each other pleasure.

"We can't fall asleep like this." He pressed himself against the length of her back and lightly kissed her neck. "I don't trust myself to wake up next to you."

Nina smiled, then reached for the hand he had resting on the hip of her unbuttoned jeans and brought it up to cover her bare breast. "You mean you're not done yet?"

"I don't think I'll ever be done." She heard a low growl in his throat—or maybe the sound came from her—as his thumb brushed across her nipple. "Which is why I need to take you home now. I'm not going to be able to stop at third base next time."

Nina giggled. "Did you just refer to what we did as third base? I'm pretty sure you didn't even call it that when we were teenagers."

"Not in front of you, I didn't." His lips moved to her shoulder. "But everyone in the locker room used to tease me about not making it to second base with you."

"We made it to second base back then." She turned to face him, and the sprinkling of dark hair on his chest tickled her breasts. "Didn't we? Second base means kissing, right?"

He ran his palms along her spine, making her shiver. "I think there's varying opinions on the subject and we definitely did plenty of kissing. But there was no way I was going to talk about any of that with my teammates, especially with Luca looking like he wanted to punch anyone who dared to bring up your name."

"Then we better not tell him how much I liked getting to third base with you." She meant for her kiss to be casual and leisurely. After all, they'd already found their own releases even if they hadn't had intercourse. However, as soon as their tongues touched, the flames of passion quickly reignited.

Nina rolled onto her back, and Barrett followed, his forearms holding his weight as the loosened end of his belt buckle clinked against her open zipper. He groaned again. "We really need to stop."

It took another thirty minutes of kissing and touching and stroking before they were dressed again and making their way down the elevator and through the empty lobby of the hotel. They weren't exactly trying to sneak out, but Nina also wasn't looking toward the front desk because she didn't want to risk making eye contact with anyone during what her friends referred to as the walk of shame.

Nina had talked a big game about not caring who saw her with Barrett and not caring about her reputation. But deep down, she knew that any gossip about her would also make its way back to her brothers and her parents. It was probably best that she spared her family from having to defend her honor, even though she knew they gladly would. After the way Luca reacted to seeing Nina and Barrett dancing together at the Social Club, it was apparent she wasn't the only Sanchez who had strong opinions about Barrett's return to Tenacity.

Barrett's truck engine sounded especially loud when he started it, probably because the rest of the small town was fast asleep this late at night. Or rather this early in the morning, she corrected herself when she saw the clock on the dash.

Neither of them spoke much as they drove, and Nina was curious if Barrett still remembered the way to get to her house. She shouldn't have been surprised that he did. They'd been neighbors, after all.

He did slow as he passed his old house, and she wanted to ask him what he was thinking. But she had a feeling that his emotions would be mixed with both good and bad memories. The one thing that couldn't be ignored, though, was how much it had changed since he'd lived there.

"The new owners painted it a few years ago," she said quietly.

"I guess it's not a rental anymore, huh?"

In a town like Tenacity, land was passed down from generation to generation and many people had their own ranches, some smaller than others. There were a few families like the Sanchezes, who had a sharecropper-type of lease agreement where the tenants lived in a modest house on the property in exchange for a percentage of the yearly revenues they made working the land. And then there were those who worked in town and didn't need the acreage—like Barrett's family.

"I think the previous owners had a tough time renting it out after you guys left."

"Why?" Barrett had completely stopped in the middle of the road, his engine idling. "Was there crime scene tape around it or something?"

"Now that you mention it, no. That's kind of weird. I remember going over there a few weeks after you left and climbing into your bedroom window. Remember how it had that jiggly latch?"

"Of course you would've broken in and done some snooping." His tone was mostly teasing, but she knew that it also held a slight reprimand. Her brothers had been livid when they'd found out their fourteen-year-old sister had gone over there to look for clues about Barrett's whereabouts. They were a Mexican-American family in a town with a predominantly white population, and her parents had raised them to be more cautious.

"I didn't break in." She told him the same thing she'd told her brothers. "I was merely assisting in the investigation."

"Without permission," Barrett corrected. He hadn't moved from where he'd stopped in the street, but it was still dark and nobody was out driving yet.

"I figured I had your permission. You were the one who showed me how to get around the latch."

The dash lights were dim, but she could see him roll his eyes. "Did you find any clues?"

"No. I was hoping for a goodbye note or maybe an encrypted message written on the back of your closet or something. But I had to make do with the only things I found hanging in there. Your favorite hoodie, which thankfully still smelled like you. And your practice jersey, which also smelled like you, but not in a good way."

Barrett's smile lit up the cab of the truck. "Then you *did* find my goodbye messages. The hoodie was for you because you would always pretend you were cold so that you could borrow it. The jersey was for Luca. But I didn't have time to wash it."

"Oh. So…um… I might not have known about sharing the jersey with my brother. I kind of kept that for myself until Marisa wouldn't stop complaining about the stench. I was at barrel-racing practice when she finally found it shoved behind our laundry hamper, so she turned it into the school since it said Property of Tenacity High on it. I was so mad, I didn't talk to her for three days."

"You probably could've just washed it." Barrett chuckled. Then his voice grew somber and he nodded toward his old house again. "So if there wasn't a big investigation, why did it sit empty for so long?"

"Oh. Um." Nina wanted to be careful not to mention the missing money because she was already sick of hearing everyone talk about how it had such a financial impact on the town. "I guess with the recession happening, there were more people leaving Tenacity than moving here. One of the high school math teachers lives there now with her kids. I think she's a single mom, but she spends a lot of time on the weekends and the summer fixing up the place."

"It definitely looks way better than it did when I lived there," he said, easing off the brake and resuming the drive to Nina's house.

When he pulled into her driveway, she was toying with the idea of inviting him inside for a cup of coffee. But there was already a light on in the kitchen window. Which meant at least one of her parents was awake and waiting for her.

"You want to come in and say hi?" she asked, knowing full well that it was the last thing Barrett wanted to do.

"Maybe we should hold off on the formal visit until we're all a bit more rested," he said rather diplomatically. She was exhausted after being awake for nearly twenty hours straight, but his normally intense brown eyes were bloodshot. She wondered when he'd last slept.

"Okay. Go back to the hotel and get some sleep. Just keep in mind that the drugstore closes early on Sundays."

"Yeah, they have their hours painted on their window. Why do you think I was going so slow when we drove by there a few minutes ago?"

Nina smiled, anticipation racing through her as she realized that he was still just as eager as she was to finish what they'd started back in his hotel room. "Then I'll see you later?"

"Don't you guys still do family dinners on Sunday?"

"Usually. Although the schedule has become more chaotic with Marisa having to drive in from Bronco with her husband and Julian and Diego bringing their fiancées and their kids, and well, it's just gotten more difficult to coordinate. Why? Do you want to come over for dinner?"

"Someday," he said noncommittally. Nina mentally kicked herself for pushing too hard, too soon. The Sanchezes were a lot, and Barrett had only been in town for two days. He was probably feeling overwhelmed.

He opened his door, and she grabbed his arm before he could get out. "You don't need to walk me. In fact, it's probably better if you stay here."

"Fine." He gave her a quick kiss—or at least it seemed quick compared to the long, lingering ones they'd shared most of the night—and even though he looked like he was going to override her, he thankfully remained in the driver's seat as she let herself out.

Don't look back at him, she warned her brain as she took the front porch steps, trying to avoid the squeaky plank that would alert whoever was in the kitchen that she was sneaking into the house before dawn. She was too exhausted to properly overthink what the past two days had meant for her, let alone what it had meant for Barrett.

Nina exhaled quietly when she bolted the front door behind her and heard her father's sound snoring from her parents' small bedroom on the other side of the living room. But her relief was short-lived when she saw her mother come out of the kitchen carrying two steaming hot cups of coffee.

Nicole Sanchez put a finger to her lips, then she took a sip out of one and passed the other to her daughter before turning to walk down the hall toward the other bedrooms, leaving Nina no choice but to follow.

Chapter Seven

Nina had unofficially gotten a room to herself when her sister moved out, but the remnants from both girls' childhood still remained. The white twin bedframes were the only things that matched in the room. Their mom was a talented seamstress and had allowed the sisters to pick out the fabric for their handmade comforters based on their own preferences. Nina's was a deep shade of purple that had faded to lavender over the years while Marisa's was ballet-slipper pink and currently served as a catchall surface for everything Nina hadn't had time to put away—like a stack of folded laundry, a shipping box containing a new autobiography of an FBI agent, and a charging laptop.

The rest of the room was strewn with awards and memorabilia from the girls' adolescence. The trophies and ribbons from junior rodeo competitions were Nina's. The dried flowers from dance recitals and a framed program from a *Swan Lake* performance were Marisa's.

Even though Nina spent many nights in the bunkhouses at whichever ranch she happened to be working on, this room had remained a comforting refuge because she could always count on the familiar space to stay the same. At this exact moment, though, she wished she would've taken the time to redecorate so that it didn't feel so…childish. Especially with her mom moving an old teddy bear off the turquoise desk chair before settling in for what was sure to be a lengthy chat.

Normally, the Sanchez family conducted their most serious conversations at the dining room table. Bedroom discussions were reserved for only the most private of matters, like when their mom had sat her preteen daughters down to explain how their bodies would be changing. Or when her dad gave her a long list of the dangers of drinking at parties before she'd left for college.

So the fact that Nicole Sanchez had chosen this space for whatever she wanted to say meant that Nina was about to feel like a child again. After carefully setting her mug on top of three yearbooks stacked on the white wicker nightstand, she sighed loudly as she collapsed dramatically onto her bed. Maybe that hadn't exactly conveyed an image of maturity, either, she decided before leaning onto a ruffled throw pillow and yawning loudly.

"Mom, I'm twenty-nine years old. I'm too old for a curfew and definitely too old for a lecture."

"Actually, you're thirty, *mija*." Her mom nodded toward the alarm clock. "You have been for four hours now. Happy birthday."

The number hit Nina with a force, and she drew in a deep, shaky breath.

Thirty.

Did she feel thirty? No. But she also didn't feel like a teenager. So where had all those years in between gone? How old was she supposed to feel?

"Is that boy coming back tonight for your birthday dinner?"

"That boy?" Nina lifted her knee to her chest so she could tug off her boot. "A second ago, you were so eager to remind me of how old I am. But now you're calling Barrett a boy."

"I'm sorry. I should have said 'that man.'" Nicole Sanchez's sarcastic tone suggested she wasn't truly apologizing. "That full-grown man who's had fifteen years to come back to Tenacity and make things right."

"He's back now." Nina yanked harder on the other boot, her grunt making her statement seem all the more defensive.

"I'm not trying to argue with you." Her mother made a tsking sound. "I just want you to be cautious of rushing into something with someone that you know nothing about."

Since Nina wasn't going to be getting any sleep anytime soon, she shifted into a sitting position and fortified herself with the coffee she hadn't wanted.

"I do too know him, Mom. And so do you. Barrett Deroy used to carpool to school with us. He came to all our birthday parties. Barrett helped set the table for our Sunday dinners and then washed dishes in our kitchen sink afterward. Dad was his soccer coach, and you taught him how to sew a button. Luca was his best friend, and I was his first—" Nina paused, then decided her mother didn't need all the specifics. "Remember that one game when the ref made a bad call and Barrett's cool composure was the only reason why most of the varsity football team, including Luca, didn't get ejected from the game for fighting?"

"I know who he used to be," her mom said, standing up and tightening the belt on her favorite robe. "But people change. Circumstances change. All I'm saying is you need to be careful."

Nina tried to rub the exhaustion and exasperation from her eyes. "Careful of what? Him leaving suddenly with no explanation? He's already done that once, and I survived."

"Of him breaking your heart again," Will Sanchez's voice came from the doorway, his salt-and-pepper hair standing up in different directions.

"Sorry for waking you up, Dad," Nina said with a grimace. Her parents were getting older and still worked as hard as they had when they were supporting a family of five kids. "I know Sundays are your only day to sleep in."

"I was getting up anyway to make my birthday girl *chilaquiles* for breakfast." He shuffled over to her bed and dropped a kiss on top of her head. "You want your eggs over easy?"

"Yes, please." Nina's stomach rumbled. When was the last time she'd eaten? She and Barrett only split an appetizer at the Social Club last night. The memory caused her to tug the collar of her very wrinkled shirt higher. "I'm going to take a shower first, though."

She might officially be thirty, but she wasn't about to sit at her parents' kitchen table wearing yesterday's eyeliner and the whisker burn from Barrett's five o'clock shadow on her collarbone.

Thankfully nobody said another word about Barrett's return for the rest of the morning. Of course, it helped that Nina fell asleep immediately after breakfast and didn't hear all the text messages popping up on her phone wishing her a happy birthday and asking what she was doing to celebrate. What everyone really wanted to know was *who* she was celebrating with.

She skipped all of those messages when she woke up later that afternoon and went straight to the most recent notification. Her heart skipped a beat and her grin widened at Barrett's text.

Happy birthday, Nina. Have a piece of strawberry cake for me.

It took every ounce of willpower she possessed not to reply with another invitation to dinner tonight. He'd already politely declined, and after her mom's lecture earlier, it was obvious that having Barrett over with all of her family wouldn't exactly be festive for everyone.

But she also wanted to celebrate with him. So she typed I'll save a piece for you and then pressed the send arrow.

Barrett was still thinking about that strawberry cake and, more importantly, how much he couldn't wait to see Nina again when he got a call from his mom on Sunday afternoon.

"Hi, Barry." Her use of the fake name made him cringe. "How is everything going in Tenacity?"

"Well, I'm not behind bars, so it's going better than expected. How are you and Dad?"

"Barry, it's me," his father responded on his own behalf. Apparently this was a speakerphone call, one of the few times his parents did anything together. "Did you see the Woodsons?"

"Can we please stop calling me Barry, now? I never liked it back then, and it's just completely unnecessary now."

Except his father didn't acknowledge his request. He continued the same train of thought. "How do they look?"

"The Woodsons?" Barrett pinched the bridge of his nose. "I only saw Brent. And he looked like he wanted to punch me."

"But what about June and Cliff?" his dad asked. "Are they around anymore?"

That seemed like an odd thing to focus on after his son

had just disclosed he'd nearly gotten into a fistfight. But since the former mayor was the one who'd made the initial accusation, Barrett supposed his dad would obviously be more worried about that potential threat.

"I haven't really asked anyone about that yet." Barrett tamped down a nudge of guilt for not doing much today to further his investigation. He had crashed when he got back to the hotel after dropping off Nina, sleeping for several hours straight. Then once he woke up and remembered it was her birthday, he spent an hour trying to find a nearby florist who would deliver on such short notice.

"Have you talked to anyone yet?" his dad asked at the same time his mom said, "Did you meet with that attorney?"

"Yes and yes," Barrett replied. "I met with the attorney yesterday and I've seen a few familiar faces. I...uh...also ran into Nina."

"Who?" his father asked.

"The neighbor lady who did all the sewing," his mother explained wrong. "She had the old minivan and all the kids. She used to take Barrett to soccer practice and bring him home from school."

"Mom, you're thinking of Nicole Sanchez. Nina is her daughter."

"Oh right, the little girl who always followed Barrett around," his dad said, and Barrett was tempted to set his phone down and let them carry on their side chat until they decided to include him. "What was her name? Nancy? Naomi?"

"Her name is Nina, Dad. I literally just said it a few moments ago when you interrupted—"

"Did you go to the grocery store yet?" His mom interrupted this time. "Does Mrs. Chen still run it?"

"I haven't needed groceries yet, Mom. I only arrived two days ago, and I'm staying at the Tenacity Inn. So I don't exactly have a kitch—"

"What about the Grizzly?" Dad asked. "Is that still there?"

"Yeah, it's still there, but I didn't go inside." Only into the parking lot behind it when he first ran into Nina. "I did go to the Tenacity Social Club, though."

"I never saw why so many people liked that place," his mom said. "Too many kids hanging around, and the bands were nothing special."

"I remember you liking one singer in particular, Macy," his father said.

"He was a poet," his mom corrected her husband as if they'd had this same conversation before. "But why would you bother taking the time to know that I like poetry?"

"You know what's wild?" Barrett hadn't realized he'd spoken aloud until he heard the silence on the other end of the line. Like his parents were finally going to listen to something he had to say. "You two have refused to talk about Tenacity for the past fifteen years. It was the one subject I could never bring up. But now that I'm here, you both suddenly want to hear about every little detail."

His mom gasped, and Barrett immediately regretted his words. Or at least the tone of his voice.

"Come on, Barry... Barrett," his father quickly corrected himself. "It's not like we ever forbade you from talking about anything."

"Dad, anytime I so much as mentioned a memory as simple as the bubble gum they used to have at the counter of the Feed and Seed, Mom would head straight to her room and you'd hightail it out of whatever apartment we were at to go to the nearest bar."

"I'm not dealing with this." His mother's words were followed by the echoing sound of retreating footsteps.

His father sighed loudly. "Now you know why we don't ever talk about Tenacity."

Barrett rolled his eyes despite the fact that his parents couldn't see him. His entire adolescence and early adulthood had been the same way. He loved his folks, but they always made him feel as though he was being confrontational when he only wanted to have what he thought was a simple conversation. No wonder Barrett preferred brooding silence to open communication.

"Listen, Dad. I wasn't trying to upset either of you. I was trying to answer your questions."

"I know, son. But you have to understand that we're concerned about you putting yourself into Woodson's crosshairs again by being there."

Really? Because it had sounded more like curiosity than concern a few moments ago. But Barrett knew better than to argue that point.

"That's the thing, Dad. You make it seem like I'm in danger. Like you know something I don't know. Yet you and Mom have never really given me any reason why everyone in Tenacity was so hell-bent on accusing me. You don't actually believe I stole the money, do you?"

"Of course not."

"Then why didn't you stay in town and fight for me?"

"You don't know Cliff Woodson like I do. He was going to do everything in his power to take you down. So I did everything in my power to keep you safe."

"In that case, you should come back to Tenacity and help me, Dad. You still know people here. You could ask them some of the same questions Nina and I plan on asking."

There was a long pause on the other end, and Barrett

held his breath, hoping his father would finally be willing to confront the past with him.

Finally, the man spoke, his voice already sounding weary and defeated. "I don't know, Barrett. I've got the Three Forks rodeo next week, which is prime time for me to make a few extra bucks shoeing horses. And even if your mother hadn't vowed to never go back to that city, she probably wouldn't want to take more than a day or two off work. I'm sure you'll be back to Whitehorn by then."

"Yeah, probably." Barrett stared up at the ceiling of his hotel room. "Listen, I'm going to run out and grab something to eat. Thanks for calling and checking in. Tell Mom I love her."

They said their goodbyes, and Barrett ended the call. He was accustomed to being alone in strange hotel rooms, but he was antsy. And he was hungry. He checked his phone to see if Nina had replied to his text. Maybe she'd invite him again and not take no for an answer this time, insisting he stop by for her birthday dinner. Then he'd feel like he wasn't just sitting here spinning his wheels.

Or maybe he should go to Tenacity Drugs & Sundries and pick up a few things just in case Nina wanted to come over later tonight. He grabbed his wallet and keys just as the hotel room phone rang.

The sound caught him by surprise since he was out of the habit of using a landline. When he finally picked up, he thought there might be a problem with the connection because nobody was there. He shrugged, put the receiver back in the cradle, and was almost out the door when it rang again.

This time when he answered, he could definitely hear someone breathing on the other end. He didn't give the caller the satisfaction of asking what they wanted. Barrett simply waited. After about thirty seconds, he heard a man's faint voice in the background of the call. "Is the pot roast ready—"

The click from the disconnect was abrupt, as if someone slammed down their phone. Whoever it was must've been calling from a landline because cell phones didn't make that sound when hung up suddenly.

It couldn't have been another guest in the hotel, Barrett thought as he left his room and made his way down the carpeted hallway. Whoever was calling wasn't being summoned for pizza delivery or for a sack of take-out burgers. Which meant someone was calling from wherever they were having Sunday dinner.

He would've chalked it up to a wrong number if the caller hadn't stayed on the line for so long. It could've just been a coincidence, but too many people still held a grudge and probably wanted to drive him out of town.

Getting answers meant asking questions. So Barrett forced himself to stop by the front desk to talk to the same teenager he'd seen vaping outside the delivery door last night. Barrett had to stand there for several seconds before the young clerk looked up from the video playing on his phone.

"Oh, hey. Did you need something?" The kid wasn't wearing a uniform, let alone a name tag, and Barrett suddenly wondered if he actually worked at the hotel. He definitely hadn't been trained in customer service.

Since nobody else was around, Barrett asked, "Did you put a call through to room two-eighteen just a few minutes ago?"

"Nah, man," the teen replied a bit sullenly, then returned his attention to the phone screen.

Barrett glanced down at the video and saw that it was

a football clip playing on a social media app. He asked, "What team is that?"

"Bronco High." The teen held the phone at an angle so Barrett could see it better. "Their tight end just posted this kickoff return one of their special-teams guys made."

"Is that from last season?" Barrett leaned in closer, noticing the players looked to be wearing practice jerseys.

"No, it's from a couple of days ago. They're already starting their preseason workouts. Tenacity High is never going to stand a chance against them this year. The district hasn't even found us a new coach yet, let alone paid to get the field reseeded and lined."

Barrett wasn't surprised to hear that the high school was in just as bad of shape as the rest of the town. "Can't someone organize informal practices at the park or something?"

"There's a few of us that have been throwing the ball around a little, and my aunt said that if I help her out at the hotel, we could possibly use the 'gym' here." The boy did air quotes. "I tried to tell her that a treadmill and some fifteen-pound dumbbells aren't going to cut it. We're athletes. We need real workout equipment."

Barrett was tempted to make a comment about the teen's underage vaping, but it wasn't really any of his business. "You don't need anything fancy to build up strength and endurance."

"I do if I want to be able to compete with this." The kid held up his phone, which had moved on to the next video reel showing a fake handoff, resulting in a sixty-yard pass for a touchdown.

"Our offensive line used to run these drills out at Hayes Parker's ranch." Barrett chuckled at the memory. "We'd use hay bales to practice our inside-zone footwork, which would trick the defense into a play-gap so our receivers could get to the outside."

"The Start of a New Day Ranch? I think Julian Sanchez owns that place now. His brother Luca played for THS the year they went to State."

"Yeah. I was on that same team."

"Wait." The boy pointed a finger at Barrett. "You're that famous quarterback who stole a bunch of money and then disappeared from town. There's a picture of you in the trophy case at the school, but someone used a pen to draw horns and…uh…other stuff that I'm sure can probably be wiped off. Anyway, my aunt said you were back in town."

As if the teen was summoning her, Carol Overton, the desk clerk who had originally checked Barrett into the Tenacity Inn, came out of the office behind the front desk.

"Hey, Aunt Carol. This is Bart Deltoid. He said me and the guys should go out to Julian Sanchez's ranch and practice our inside footwork with some hay bales."

Okay, that wasn't exactly what Barrett had said. Although he had to admit that the mistaken alias could've been much worse. Being called by the wrong name was better than having his picture defaced.

"You mean Barrett Deroy," Carol corrected her nephew, who was already focused on his phone and tapping on the screen. She shook her head before speaking to Barrett. "Sorry about Grayson. He's a little football obsessed. Anyway, a woman called for you earlier. I transferred the call to your room, but it must not have gone through the first time because she called back right away."

Barrett's curiosity was piqued now that he remembered why he'd stopped by the front desk in the first place. "Did they say who it was?"

"No, Mr. Deroy. And I know everyone in town and would've recognized their voice if it was someone local."

"They could've been disguising their voice," the nephew said. "My friend Caden has an app on his phone that lets you do that."

"Is that the kid who's been selling you the vape cartridges?"

"No, that's…" The teenager's eyes went wide. "How did you know about those, Aunt Carol?"

"Because I saw the empty box in the breakroom trash can and I know they aren't anyone else's who works here."

"You're not gonna tell my mom, are you?"

Carol was the last person Barrett would've trusted with a secret, but clearly her nephew still had hope.

"Not if you show up on time every day this week and help with housekeeping."

"But Mr. Deltoid said we should be practicing on our own since we don't have a coach yet. I wanted to get the guys together to meet him and run some plays."

"What time were you planning to hold this practice of yours?" Carol asked Barrett.

"Me?" Barrett's brows slammed together. "I wasn't planning on holding anything. I was only suggesting—"

The desk phone rang, and Carol held up a finger as she answered it immediately. "Thank you for calling the Tenacity Inn. How may I help you?"

Barrett's mind snapped to the call that had been transferred to his room.

"It's Caden's mom." Carol didn't bother to put her hand over the receiver to mute the call. "She wants to know what time practice is tomorrow."

Barrett's neck stretched forward, trying to angle his

ear closer because surely he'd misheard something. "What practice?"

Grayson held up his screen. "The one I just told the guys about in the group chat."

Oh hell. How had this happened? How had Barrett been mistaken for an actual football coach? He was about to explain that he had absolutely no intention of helping a bunch of teenage boys get ready for the fall season when the front desk phone rang again. Carol put Caden's mom on hold and answered another line.

"Yes, Jocelyn. It's *that* Barrett Deroy. The same one you wouldn't wait on yesterday at the Silver Spur." Carol paused long enough that Barrett could only imagine what the server was saying about him on the other end. Then Carol spoke again. "Well, you can carry a grudge if you want to, Jocelyn, but I've seen your son kick the football and our boys will need some field goals if we're going to stand a chance against Bronco High this year... Uh-huh... Uh-huh... Well, let me find out what time he wants them at practice, and I'll call you back."

If Barrett hadn't already been so skilled at controlling his emotions, his mouth would be wide open in shock at the recent development. He should've remembered how seriously some of the people of Tenacity took their football. Almost as serious as they took cowboying. And if parents were willing to entrust him with their impressionable teenagers, then maybe they'd entrust him with some answers that could clear his name.

But he wasn't trained to coach football. He also wasn't trained to investigate a fifteen-year-old cold case involving stolen money, yet he was already committed to that. How many kids would show up anyway? Three? Five at the most? It shouldn't be all that tough. He'd run them through some hard drills, and they probably wouldn't even show up the next day.

When he saw that both Grayson and his aunt were looking at him expectantly, Barrett swallowed a groan and said, "Tell them to be there at three o'clock tomorrow."

"Where?" Grayson asked. "At the ranch?"

"Not yet." Barrett certainly hadn't spoken with Julian yet, and he doubted Nina could talk her brother into letting a group of boys and an accused thief use his property. "Let's meet at the park tomorrow and see what comes of it."

Carol and Grayson both got distracted passing along the information, and Barrett quickly left the hotel lobby before he got roped into teaching an art class as well. Ugh. This had to be the worst idea Barrett had ever had. There was no way this wasn't going to completely backfire on him.

Chapter Eight

"This has to be the most brilliant idea you've ever had," Nina said when she walked up to the makeshift sideline where Barrett was dumping out a netted bag full of brand-new footballs. It was a quarter to three on Monday afternoon, and there were already at least eight boys and one girl setting up orange cones in the park.

"I assure you it is not." Barrett frowned behind his dark sunglasses.

Nina nodded to where several parents were stationed at a wobbly picnic table, chatting with each other as they watched their children. "When you texted me the plan last night, I knew this would be way more productive than driving all over town looking for people who would talk to us. You're about to have everyone coming right to you and dropping information in our laps."

"A lot of good that will do when I can't even talk to them. I spent the entire morning researching football drills online. Then I realized that I didn't even own a football. I called the high school to see if they'd let us use some equipment, but the office was closed for summer break."

"So then where did you get this stuff?"

"A sporting goods store in Lewiston."

"You drove all the way to Lewiston today?"

"No. I was busy watching lateral shuffles on YouTube. Marshall picked them up for me."

"Your attorney?" Nina asked.

"Yeah. He had to get some new clothes anyway. Besides, I had already driven to Bronco last night."

"Bronco?" Nina lifted one brow. "I know you used to like going to Cubbie's, Barrett, but we do sell ice cream at the grocery store here in town."

In fact, Nina wanted to ask him if he'd made it to Tenacity Drugs & Sundries before it closed yesterday. But another teenager was walking from the parking lot toward them.

"I was going stir crazy and needed to clear my head." Barrett lowered his voice and whispered into her ear, "Plus, their drugstore is open later."

Nina's cheeks suddenly went warm. So she wasn't the only one still thinking about spending more time together. The fact that he had made a special trip to go buy condoms was a good sign. And judging by how many onlookers were watching this impromptu football practice, it was probably best that he hadn't made any personal purchases in town causing people to talk about them more than they already were.

She cleared her throat. "Well, I'm going to let you do your thing here while I head over to that side of the park to see if anyone knows something."

"Good luck," he said as a pack of high schoolers headed his way. "I don't know which one of us has the tougher job."

"Definitely you," she called out over her shoulder as she walked away. Nina was still wearing the jeans and boots that she'd worn to work today. She'd thought about taking the week off to focus on Barrett and the investigation she'd initiated, but she was so close to getting Gladiator, a beautiful Arabian stallion, to trust her and if she didn't show up for their normal routine, she might have to start from scratch again. Besides, it was better this way. It would draw less attention to what they were doing if she followed her same daily routine and then met up with Barrett in the afternoons and evenings to go over things.

Or at least that was what she'd thought before more people started showing up at the park to watch him direct a bunch of teenagers through stretches and warm-ups. He even ran a few laps around the park with them.

Everyone there was watching intently.

"I thought he looked good in his jeans and boots, but those athletic shorts he's wearing make me wonder things I shouldn't be wondering," one of the moms said, and Nina had to remind herself not to get jealous. Barrett had always been attractive, even if he was younger than most of these women.

"Makes me want to know where he stashed all that cash," another woman said. "Because I'm pretty sure he was wearing those same shorts the day he stopped by town hall. It was right after that when the money and his family went missing."

Nina wasn't about to let the old rumors gain any traction, though, so she spoke up. "I guarantee you that Barrett never owned a pair of shorts like that fifteen years ago. See the Grizzlies emblem above the hem? That's from the University of Montana. He had his heart set on Wyoming when he was younger and never would have worn something from a rival school."

"Well, you would know," said another mom. Jocelyn from the Silver Spur.

The waitress's snarky response put Nina on the defensive, but she needed to keep the other woman talking. "How do you know he was at town hall the day the money went missing?"

"I didn't say he was there that day. Just that we couldn't find the money after that."

"That's right, Bridget," Carol said. "I forgot you worked at town hall around that time."

"I wonder what a sixteen-year-old was doing at town hall." Nina tried to make it sound like she was simply thinking aloud. She knew that too many questions might come across as an interrogation.

"He was with his dad. If you think Barrett Junior is good looking, you should've seen his old man. All the ladies would giggle and fall over themselves whenever Barrett Senior stopped by to renew his business license."

"So his dad was there to renew his business license?" Nina suddenly wondered how many other people were in and out of town hall on any given day.

"I think so." Bridget tilted her head for a few moments. "Yeah, I'm pretty positive that's why he was there that day. You know who would probably know for sure? June Woodson. She used to process paperwork for the city clerk and would always help him."

The subject quickly turned to job openings at town hall, which led to a conversation about getting more people to move to Tenacity and then someone asked about Marshall Gordon and whether the new attorney practiced family law. That led to several side conversations about other people who might or might not have relationship issues, and Nina got an ache in her neck as her head pivoted back and forth trying to keep up with all the gossip.

When the kids took a water break, Nina walked over to where Cecil Brewster and Otis Corey were sitting on a bench. She was hoping to get some insight from the older men, but they were too busy reliving their own glory days from when they used to play for Tenacity High.

Nina pretended not to notice that Luca was standing under the shade of a tree, his arms crossed over his chest as he watched. She had expected a big lecture from her family last night at dinner, but with Ruby and Jenna there with their kids, everyone was focused on other things. Thankfully.

Ignoring Luca's presence was one thing. But it was more difficult for her to act like she didn't see Brent Woodson's truck slowly drive down Central Avenue and then park across the street. Nina hoped the man didn't make a scene or cause any problems for Barrett. Things might have gotten a little heated on the Fourth of July, but it wasn't like Brent was some sort of villain. Of course, she'd also been completely oblivious to how bitter the rivalry had been between him and Barrett growing up.

She knew the exact moment that Barrett spotted Brent because he'd gone from laughing with one of the boys who was trying to show off his end-zone dance to barking out instructions for the next drill.

Luca must have also noticed because her brother shifted his position so that he could see both the practice and Brent's truck. If something went down, Luca would be in the best position to intervene, so Nina decided to go stand by him.

"Why didn't you mention last night that Barrett was a football coach?" Luca asked.

"Because as far as I know, he isn't one."

Luca jerked one side of his mouth upward. "Well, he doesn't suck at it."

"I'm sure he'd appreciate your positive feedback." Nina

rolled her eyes, but her brother wasn't paying any attention to her.

"Woodson is in his truck watching."

"I saw that." Nina's tone wasn't quite as nonchalant. "Do you think he'll cause any trouble?"

"Would you blame him if he did?" Luca asked.

"Of course I would," she replied quickly. "You can't tell me that you'd take his side over Barrett's?"

"Nobody needs to take sides, Nina."

"Everybody has already taken sides, Luca."

"Well, they shouldn't."

"That's a brilliant idea. Nobody should have an opinion. Everyone should mind their own business. I wonder why the rest of the people in town haven't already thought of that." Nina tapped her chin dramatically. "Oh, I know why. Because they're not new here."

"Anyone ever tell you that your sarcasm can be so annoying, Nina?"

"Only my big brothers. Hey, do you remember that smelly old football jersey Barrett used to wear for practices?"

Luca's mouth turned to a thin, clenched line. "What about it?"

"Apparently he purposely left it behind for you the night his family took off."

He uncrossed his arms, then crossed them again. There was a slight ticking of the muscle above his jaw. "How do you know?"

"Because I saw it hanging next to his favorite hoodie when I snuck into his house back then to search for clues." She held up her palm. "Save the lecture. Barrett already gave me one. Anyway, his parents didn't want him writing any goodbye letters, so he left those instead. Except I didn't know the jersey was meant for you."

When her brother didn't respond right away, she realized that he was lost in his own thoughts. And Nina was dying to know what those were. "Is there something special about that jersey?"

"Nah. It was just a practice jersey."

"Then what was the significance of him leaving it for you?"

"You ask way too many questions, Nina."

"Or maybe you don't ask enough questions," she challenged him back.

"Here's a question that I'll never figure out the answer for." Luca's mischievous smirk was back. "What could Barrett possibly see in a mouthy little tagalong like you?"

She tried to playfully shove her brother's arm, but he was already walking toward the huddle where Barrett was talking to the players. Before she could catch up to him, she was waylaid by a text from her mom.

Will you be home for dinner tonight?

No. She wrote back. Thank you for checking, though.

They hadn't discussed it yet, but Nina was hoping Barrett would be taking her to dinner.

"What did my brother say to you after practice?" Nina asked Barrett as they sat in a wooden booth across from each other at Castillo's Mexican Restaurant.

"He said that I should bring the kids out to Julian's ranch next week to practice inside-zone footwork with the hay bales."

"Will you?" she asked.

"That's not why I'm in town. I don't plan on staying any longer than necessary, and I don't want anyone to get attached."

What Nina heard was that he didn't want *her* to get attached. That was fine. He was here now, and she would have to make the most of it.

"Speaking of why you're in town, I heard something interesting today," Nina started, but Yolanda Castillo, who owned the restaurant with her husband, arrived at their table to take their orders.

"I was starting to wonder when you were going to stop by and see us," the older woman said to Barrett. "I told Pablo you wouldn't be able to stay away from our homemade *buñuelos*."

Barrett smiled and patted his stomach. "I've been thinking about them for fifteen years."

"Then you can wait another hour for them. You need to eat real food first." The woman turned to Nina. "You want corn or flour tortillas tonight?"

"Let's do both," Nina replied.

Yolanda picked up the untouched menus and returned to the kitchen. Barrett leaned across the narrow table and whispered, "Don't we need to order something other than tortillas and *buñuelos*?"

"Don't be silly, Barrett. I've been coming here since I was a little girl. Yolanda knows I always get the fajitas."

"But she doesn't know what I always get."

"The enchiladas suizas?" Nina smiled when she saw the expression on Barrett's face and knew she'd guessed correctly. "My mom still hasn't made those for our family since that one time."

Barrett's cheeks went slightly pink. "How was I supposed to know that she'd take it as an insult when I asked if she wanted Mr. Castillo to give her his recipe?"

"You suggested it *after* tasting my mom's."

"I was twelve, and my own mom relied on frozen and precooked meals she could bring home from the grocery store. I figured since both your mother and Mr. Castillo liked to make the same thing, she might have a little more success with his recipe."

Nina tried to hold back a laugh but couldn't. "Well, let's just say that anytime the Castillos bring enchiladas to a potluck, my brothers have a field day asking my mom if she wants to try a bite."

When Yolanda returned to the table with the chips and salsa, the front door opened, and Uncle Stanley and Winona walked inside. Nina had always loved the cozy feel of the restaurant with its narrow storefront, dim lighting, and two rows of wooden booths. However, when the older couple took the table closest to Nina and Barrett, Nina's hope for a romantic dinner quickly diminished. But she forced a smile on her face as everyone made the necessary greetings and small talk.

Apparently, Winona was trying to learn more Spanish, so Stanley and Yolanda coached her as she placed her order, and Barrett held back a grin when the woman accidentally asked for Fritos instead of frijoles.

Yolanda went to speak to her oldest son, who was tending the small bar in back, and Uncle Stanley leaned closer to their table, which was only separated by two feet. "I heard there was a good turnout for football practice today. Did you learn anything new?"

"I learned that half of the team should spend more time practicing plays instead of watching them on social media. The O line is going to need to read the defensive plays better if they expect to protect the quarterback when he's in the pocket."

"He means the investigation, Barrett," Nina explained, then turned to her great-uncle. "I found out something interesting today. Bridget used to work at town hall and made a comment about Barrett and his dad coming in shortly before the money went missing."

"So now there are witnesses placing me at the scene of the crime?" Barrett scrubbed the lower half of his face with his hand. "That doesn't exactly help my case much, does it?"

"Maybe it does," Uncle Stanley replied. "Did the city keep any sort of records or logs back then?"

"I have no idea." Barrett's shoulders lifted in a shrug. "I'm trying to remember why we went there in the first place."

"Bridget said your dad was renewing his business license. Which means there should be a record of that transaction. But more importantly, it confirms that other people routinely go in and out of town hall for any number of reasons and would have also had access to the money as well."

"I always thought that was odd." Winona pushed a stack of bracelets higher on her thin forearm, causing a melodic jingling sound. The psychic, with her long, flowing skirts and straight white hair parted down the middle, marched to her own beat when it came to style. She was a gentle soul and known for making quirky observations that seemed odd at first, but Nina had learned to listen to her insights. "Why would anyone leave so much cash sitting around town hall?"

"Good point." The wrinkles on Stanley's forehead deepened. "I'm sure there would've been a reason to have some cash on hand since people need to pay for parking tickets and water bills and stuff. But a large sum like that? I would think they'd have it locked up in a safe. Or better yet, deposited in the bank like they do now."

"It might be worth looking into," Nina suggested, even though the thought of pouring through archived records sounded like an overwhelming task that might not provide any new clues.

Their food arrived, with Nina's sizzling platter of fajitas stealing the show. The restaurant wasn't at full capacity since it was a weeknight, but there were several customers who turned in their direction. Once again, she wasn't helping Barrett keep a low profile.

"Do you ever order anything that doesn't come in a cast-iron skillet?" Barrett teased after Yolanda set down an accompanying platter of beans and rice, an assortment of toppings, and a basket of warm tortillas. "Or that isn't intended to feed a family of four?"

"Uh-oh." Uncle Stanley nodded toward Barrett's plate filled with creamy chicken enchiladas topped with a traditional green sauce. "You'd better not let my nephew's wife see you eating that."

The way Barrett's head whipped around to make sure Nina's mom hadn't just walked in was actually comical.

"Don't worry." Nina smiled. "I'm sure she's forgiven you by now."

"I know it might be tough for Luca and your parents to believe," Barrett started, "but I'm trying to get back in your family's good graces."

"Well, you're certainly back in Pablo's good graces." Nina pointed toward the kitchen, where the owner was giving Barrett a thumbs-up. "He probably can't wait to tell Cecil so that he'll accidentally say something at the Tenacity Quilting Club."

"That's another good place to gather some intelligence,"

Stanley added before reaching over and helping himself to their chips and salsa. At this point, her great-uncle and his wife might as well scoot over and join them.

Which was what they did. The rest of the meal would've felt like an awkward double date if Uncle Stanley hadn't kept the conversation focused on his plan of attack for investigating who else had been at town hall the day the money went missing and why there'd been so much cash left unattended.

Yolanda, true to her word, waited until Barrett had finished eating before bringing him a plate of warm *buñuelos*, the soft dough fried and smothered in cinnamon and sugar.

"Let me finish my coffee, *mija*." Uncle Stanley held up the mug that Yolanda had delivered with the dessert. "And then Winona and I'll give you a ride home."

Nina blinked in surprise at the offer. It was certainly kind but not exactly how she'd hoped her night would end. "Don't worry about me, Uncle Stanley. I don't need a ride."

"But your brother said Big Betty is out of commission."

"She is, sadly. But I'm using one of the trucks from Forrester Farms this week."

"That old behemoth parked out front?" Her great-uncle shook his head. "I don't trust it not to break down. We'll follow behind you just to make sure."

Nina narrowed her eyes. She knew exactly what the older man was up to. She would've accused her family of putting the idea into his head, except she knew nobody—including his physician and most local highway patrol officers—wanted Uncle Stanley out on the road more than was necessary.

Barrett wiped the sugar and cinnamon off his fingers and straightened his shoulders. "I can make sure Nina gets home, sir."

"I'm sure you can, son." Uncle Stanley took a casual sip

of his coffee. Clearly not in any hurry. "But I'll be following my niece home all the same."

Nina wadded up her napkin under the table, smiling politely even though she wanted to argue and insist that she didn't need a chaperone. She could see the determined look in her great-uncle's eyes and the equally sympathetic look in Winona's.

So much for going back to Barrett's hotel room tonight.

Chapter Nine

The rest of the week continued in much the same way. Barrett would spend his mornings phoning in to check on his ranch, then doing research or talking to his attorney about the investigation, followed by drawing up some drills and plays for the football practice that seemed to have grown in terms of both players and spectators.

Nina showed up to the park when she finished working with Gladiator, ready to socialize with anyone who could provide her with information or possible new leads. Afterward, they would go to dinner and inevitably someone from her family would show up unannounced to make sure Nina went straight home afterward and not back to Barrett's hotel.

Tuesday night had been Luca who tagged along with them to the Silver Spur Café because he wanted to talk football. Last night, Barrett had tried a different strategy to get Nina alone and away from the prying eyes of Tenacity by driving them all the way to his favorite burger place in Bronco, only to have her cousin Dylan, the one who'd given her Big Betty, insist she come by his car dealership to check out a used SUV someone had just traded in. Dylan then suggested she test drive it for the rest of the week, which was generous, but also meant they had to drive back to Tenacity separately, with Nina going straight home because Mr. Sanchez wasn't going to be satisfied until he could take a look under the hood himself.

By Thursday, Barrett knew that if he didn't get to kiss Nina soon, he was going to explode. But when he scanned the parking lot to see if she'd arrived at the park yet, he saw someone else watching practice.

Apparently, Brent Woodson no longer felt the need to keep his distance by spying on Barrett from across the street. The guy was arrogantly crossing the makeshift field and approaching the sideline.

Before Barrett could demand to know what Brent was doing there, his rival clapped his hands twice. "Looking good, Grayson. Try moving your left foot first, then juking right."

"Thanks, Mr. Woodson," the boy replied.

Barrett's fingers dug into his palms as he reminded himself not to make a scene in front of a bunch of impressionable teenagers. Instead, he spoke through a clenched jaw. "I don't remember inviting you to practice, Woodson."

"You're not the only one who played for the championship team, Deroy."

"Yeah, but if you were so dedicated to the game and coaching the fine youth of Tenacity, why didn't you throw your name in the hat for the coaching position at the high school when it opened up?"

"Because some of us have been busy living our actual lives and dealing with our actual responsibilities. Not everyone has the luxury of running away when things get too rough for them." Brent clapped twice again. "Nice footwork, Caden. Keep your arms out wider next time."

"Speaking of actual responsibilities, do you have a real job yet, or are you still coasting on your daddy's name?" Barrett asked, then raised his voice to correct his player.

"Your arms are wide enough, Caden. You just need your elbows higher."

"But not too high," Brent shouted, causing Caden to pause and look at them in confusion. The kid playing defensive tackle seized the opportunity to knock the ball out of the distracted boy's hands.

Barrett wished he was holding a clipboard right now so that he could swing it at Brent's head. "Stop trying to coach my players."

"I will as soon as you start coaching them the right way."

"The right way? I suppose if I was hoping to produce a team of second-string quarterbacks, then I might be in need of your expertise. But until then—"

"Give it a rest, you two," Luca Sanchez interrupted from behind them. "Everyone is watching this little pissing contest of yours, and it's a lot less mature now than it was back in high school."

"There was never any contest," Brent replied to Luca, but he was staring directly at Barrett. "Not fifteen years ago and certainly not now."

"Then why don't you both start acting like it?" Luca suggested. "My great-uncle isn't here to break up another fistfight. Although I am half tempted to let you two knock some sense into each other."

If Barrett had any question about his former best friend's loyalty, it certainly wasn't going to be answered today. He shook his head at Luca. "Why are you protecting him? You really think he changed that much since high school?"

"I think we've all changed since high school," Luca replied. Then he jerked his chin toward a group of boys who were aiming their rear ends at each other and making loud flatulence noises. "Thankfully."

Brent made a scoffing sound. "If I were stuck in the past, I wouldn't be here helping Deroy."

"If you really wanted to help me, Woodson, you'd admit that I wasn't the one who stole that money."

Brent shrugged. "I only know what I was told."

"You were also told that Nina was my girlfriend, but that didn't stop you from trying to steal her."

"Did I try to *steal* her, Deroy? Or did I give Nina the opportunity to improve her taste in men when you ran away and left her behind?"

"Keep my sister's name out of this argument." Luca's already cool tone dropped at least twenty degrees.

"Relax, Sanchez," Brent said. "Nobody wants your sister anymore."

Barrett's blood shot up twenty degrees hotter. But before he could defend her, Nina appeared out of nowhere.

Brent at least had the humility to turn a few shades redder and cleared his throat. "I didn't mean it to sound like that, Nina. All I was saying is that any interest I used to have was short-lived and left behind in high school. I'm sure there's *someone* out there that might want you."

"Thanks for the vote of confidence, Brent." Nina gave a sarcastic thumbs-up, and Barrett didn't know if she could be any more attractive than when she was clearly taking his side.

In an effort to prove that there was in fact someone who still wanted her, Barrett draped a protective arm around Nina's shoulders.

Unfortunately, she quickly sidestepped and gave them all a pointed look. "You three are making a scene. Cecil and Otis are over there taking bets on which one of you is going to throw the first punch."

"I'm not making a scene," Luca immediately defended

himself. "I came over to calm things down, and they dragged me into their ongoing feud."

"A feud? Really?" Brent rolled his eyes. "That would imply that I cared enough about Deroy to have given him a single thought. And I assure you that I haven't."

"Hey, Coach," Grayson called out from the center of the practice area. "Do you want us to keep running the same play, or should we take a water break?"

It was the first time someone had ever called Barrett "Coach," and he wasn't sure how he felt about the unearned title. He didn't want to give anyone false hope that he was sticking around, but at the same time, he enjoyed the satisfaction of having it reaffirmed in front of Brent that he was the one calling the shots.

"Let's take five," Barrett announced to the group, walking away from Woodson and an old argument that would never be resolved.

Nina hadn't wanted to shake off Barrett's arm when he'd put it around her shoulders in the park earlier. However, she wasn't going to let herself be used in some petty squabble to prove a point. Sure, Barrett had been openly affectionate with her when they'd been dancing at the Tenacity Social Club several days ago. But other than that, he hadn't made any physical gestures toward her in public until he decided to lay claim to her during his argument with Brent Woodson a couple of hours ago.

She'd been hoping that she and Barrett could finally be alone tonight and take food back to his hotel room where nobody in her family could show up unexpectedly. Unfortunately, one of the parents arrived at the park with a stack of pizza boxes while another one brought cupcakes, turning the football practice into an impromptu birthday party for two of the players.

Brent didn't look like he was going to leave anytime soon, which meant there was no way Barrett was going to walk away first, and Nina had to wonder if this whole coaching thing wasn't for the team or even for the investigation. Maybe he was only staying in town as a way to stick it to the Woodsons.

There was limited seating at the park since broken benches and picnic tables had been hauled off years ago and were never replaced. She tried to move from group to group while eating a slice of pepperoni pizza. However, nobody was really talking about Barrett or the missing money. At least not in front of her.

Maybe there was nothing left to say about the subject. Or maybe her fellow townspeople were starting to think she was a narc. Really, there was no reason for her to come to practices every day when she didn't have a kid on the team. And even though she and Barrett had kept their hands to themselves in public—not counting their dance at the Social Club—people had definitely seen them eating meals together and driving around in his truck. Did they think she was some sort of spy, and now they were guarding their words around her?

As she listened to Caden's mom telling the story about Corky's last grooming appointment with Renee Trent's mobile grooming business, Nina watched Barrett stand apart from the adults and only socialize with the players. And even that couldn't really be considered socializing since he seemed to be mostly listening to whatever teenage gossip they were saying and then nodding his head occasionally.

Nina grabbed another slice of pizza on her way to go stand with him so he wouldn't seem so out of his element.

But before she made her way over there, Barrett pulled out his phone and walked toward the parking lot as he answered a call. She could see the tension in his shoulders as he paced back and forth, occasionally looking up at the sky and then shoving a hand through his hair.

"He sure seems edgy," Mel Hastings said. Before Nina could swallow the pizza she was chewing, the owner of Tenacity Feed and Seed added, "He never used to be like that."

"I think he's got a lot going on." Nina took a gulp of her lemonade. "I know I'd be stressed if I was trying to clear my name of something I didn't do."

"What does he do for work nowadays?"

"He has a horse ranch in Whitehorn."

Mel whistled. "My cousin just bought fifty acres out there. It wasn't exactly cheap. I wonder where Deroy got the money for his."

Nina sensed where this conversation was headed, but it wasn't like she could offer any insight on Barrett's current financial situation. He'd never discussed it with her. Even if she did know, she wouldn't disclose it to Mel Hastings or anyone else.

"His truck is pretty new, too," he pointed out.

"Well, clearly he didn't buy it with the money we found out on Juniper Road." Nina silently congratulated herself on her word choice. Calling it missing money suggested someone stole it. But *found money* implied that it was only misplaced, hence there was no crime for anyone to be accused of.

"You watch a lot of true crime shows, right?" Mel asked but didn't wait for Nina's answer. "I was watching this one about a woman who was embezzling money from the banks where she worked. The first time she snuck a few hundred dollar bills from the drawer, held on to it for the rest of her shift, and then put it back when she left."

"Why'd she do that?" Nina asked, already regretting what Mel was going to say.

"To see if she could. When they interviewed her in prison, she said she had to teach herself how to be a thief and work her way up to the bigger jobs."

"So you think Barrett was just practicing here in Tenacity before embarking on a career as a successful thief with a horse ranch as his cover story?"

"Oh, no," Mel replied a little too quickly. "I don't know anything about his life nowadays. None of us do. But do you ever notice how in those true crime documentaries, there's always someone who thought there was no way their friend or neighbor or spouse could be capable of whatever it was they were accused of?"

Nina opened her mouth to reply but couldn't find the words. She was too busy overthinking everything the feed-store owner had just said. And why he'd said it specifically to her. Nina was about to ask him as much, but it was too late.

"Oh look, they're passing out the cupcakes." Mel hustled away, leaving Nina wondering if she was the person who was too close, the person who should've seen it coming and hadn't. Was she letting her feelings for Barrett cloud her judgment?

Nope. She shook her head to clear her mind. She'd had fifteen years of distance from Barrett. Fifteen years to let all sorts of suspicions sink in. If she'd ever doubted him, the perfect time to do so would have been when he wasn't around to defend himself. But she didn't doubt him back then and she didn't doubt him today.

Just to be sure she wasn't reliving her youth through rose-colored glasses, though, maybe it wouldn't be a bad idea to see Barrett on his own turf. Or at least on his new turf. Mel Hastings had brought up a good point that none of them really knew what Barrett's life was like nowadays. Not that he needed to provide her with any proof that he was who he said he was. Because she trusted him, Nina reminded herself as he shoved his phone into his pocket and walked toward her.

Still.

It would be nice to see things with her own eyes. To be able to add a layer of validation to that trust she'd so easily bestowed upon him. Fortunately, or at least coincidentally, the opportunity all but fell into her lap.

"I just got off the phone with my neighbor," Barrett explained. "He said there's a pretty bad water leak in my stable and several stalls are flooded. He's got the horses moved for now, but I'm going to need to drive out there tomorrow morning to meet with a plumber and help clean up."

Nina offered him the last slice of pizza on her plate and waited until his mouth was full to say, "I was planning to take off tomorrow anyway since Gladiator has a vet appointment. Since it sounds like you could use another set of hands, why don't I come to Whitehorn with you?"

She told herself that she wasn't inviting herself on his trip because Mel Hastings's words had her doubting Barrett. It was simply because she was curious to see what his life was like now. She also told herself that this was going to be one of those times that she didn't take no for an answer.

They left before dawn the following morning to make the long drive to Whitehorn. Barrett was understandably concerned about his ranch and wanted to get there right away, so breakfast was a quick drive-through off the highway. But the conversation flowed and the scenery outside the truck windows reminded Nina of why she never wanted to live anywhere outside of Montana.

Even though Nina was driving through the town of Whitehorn for the very first time, she experienced a sense of peace settle over her. "I feel like this is how Tenacity could be if we could only attract more people and businesses."

"Funny you should say that," Barrett replied. "I had the same thought when my parents and I first passed through here."

"So this was one of the places where you stopped when you were…"

"On the run?" Barrett said the words she hadn't wanted to say. "Yep. We spent a couple of nights at a motel here. It was a little too close to the police station, so we didn't stay for long. But after college, I knew I wanted to come back here."

He pointed out some of his favorite restaurants, his bank, and where he bought hardware supplies for his ranch. "We'll probably need to go there once we get to my place and see how bad the damage is. There's the grocery store where my mom works, although she's only part-time now. That's my parents' apartment. I left them a message last night telling them we were coming, so my dad's probably out at the ranch already."

Barrett's voice grew more animated, his tone more lighthearted, as he spoke about different people and landmarks they passed. Nina studied him and realized that for the first time in a week, he actually seemed relaxed. He was finally comfortable. Whitehorn was his home now. She felt an ache at what could have been if only he'd stayed in Tenacity all those years ago. If only he'd made his home with her.

No. She wasn't going to force her own point of view into

this new world of his. She was simply here to observe and learn about who he'd become.

Three miles outside of town, he turned onto a dirt road with a sign so small, she didn't even catch the name. They drove another mile and came to a T in the road. To the left was a driveway with a sign that said Bar None. Barrett went right and drove under the log-hewn sign that welcomed her to the Double N.

Her head felt a little dizzy, and she asked, "Did you come up with the name for your ranch?"

"Yeah, why?" He hugged the shoulder of the long driveway to avoid getting stuck in the wide swath of fresh mud lining the other side. Barrett hissed when they bounced over a big pothole. "Manny sent me some pictures, but I didn't realize the leak was this bad."

Nina should've shown more concern about the mess they were driving toward, but she couldn't stop herself from asking, "Is there a special meaning behind the Double N?"

"If I say yes, are you going to read too much into it?"

"Probably," she said. Yet his response was all the confirmation she needed. She'd always complained that her middle name was the same as her mom's. But Barrett, who was a junior, used to tell her that at least she got her own first name.

Nina Nicole. He once called her his Double N.

First, she'd found out that her birthday was the passcode for his phone, and now this? She couldn't stop the well of hope that bubbled inside of her. Whoops. Maybe that was a bad comparison, Nina thought, when she saw water bubbling from the ground outside the stable when they finally parked.

The bubbling water also made her realize that she hadn't

used the restroom since they'd stopped for breakfast, and Nina said as much to Barrett.

"Use the one inside the house," he said, then handed her his key. "I'm going to look around out here first."

In addition to the stables, there was a barn that appeared to be converted into some sort of garage and storage building. A log cabin with a huge wraparound porch sat on the other side of the shaded yard. His house wasn't much bigger than the one she'd grown up in, but when she let herself inside the front door, it felt larger simply by the fact that there wasn't as much furniture. The living room had a plain denim-colored sofa, a worn leather recliner, and a flat-screen television mounted over the fireplace. There were no decorative throw pillows, no lap blankets, no framed photos. There were none of the usual things that would make a house a home.

She made her way down the hall and found a restroom. After she was done, she was tempted to explore the rest of the house. However, she didn't want Barrett to think she was snooping. Hopefully, there'd be time for a tour later.

She pocketed the keys and didn't bother locking the front door behind her as she crossed the wide porch and headed across the yard to where Barrett was standing with a much older—and rugged—version of Marshall Gordon.

"Nina, this is Marshall's grandfather, Manny Gordon." Barrett made the introductions. "Manny, this is Nina Sanchez, my friend from Tenacity."

Nina held back a wince at his description. Or at least she thought she did.

"You're not his friend?" The older man had an East Coast accent and a way of studying Nina in a way that made her want to immediately divulge all of her secrets.

"Technically, I'm still his girlfriend." She chuckled awkwardly, trying to make it sound like she was joking. "We never officially broke up."

Manny's assessing gaze was textbook interrogator, but she must've answered correctly because after only a few seconds of taking her measure, he cracked a smile. "Then you two already have me beat. My longest relationship was with my second ex-wife, Marshall's grandma. And that only lasted seven years."

"Barrett told me that you're a retired NYPD detective."

"Which explains why I'm twice divorced. I was married to my job."

"And now he's married to his ranch," Barrett said, and the older man laughed.

Manny took off his cowboy hat and scratched his receding hairline. "Yeah, but I feel like I'm cheating on the Bar None considering how much time I've spent over here lately on the Double N."

"I can't tell you how much I appreciate that, Manny."

"After everything you've done for me?" the neighbor told Barrett with a dismissive wave. "Forget about it."

As the men talked, it became clear that Manny was the quintessential no-nonsense New Yorker who didn't pull any punches. He gave his opinion on everything from the work ethic of the of the college kids Barrett had hired for the summer (one of them wasn't a total idiot, but the other one couldn't find his way out of a paper bag), the local sanitation department (which was confusing the hell out of everyone with their new green waste bins that were bright orange), and the lack of a proper bagel shop in Whitehorn (the bakery did the best they could, but would it kill them to serve lox?).

The stables weren't anything fancy on the outside. But when they went inside to look at the damaged stalls, Nina saw where the real investment was. Barrett had nineteen horses, and they were all beauties. She didn't have to ask to know that their lineage was from a registered bloodline. Except for one that was exceptionally large and primarily for more heavy duty work like pulling carriages and plows. "Is that a Belgian Draught?"

"She ain't much to look at, but Big Betty's a sturdy ol' gal." Manny stroked the shaggy, wiry black mane that wouldn't win any show competitions. "I used to ride one that looked exactly like her when I was in the mounted unit before I became a detective."

"Big Betty?" Nina lifted the corner of her mouth.

"Now, *that* one is a total coincidence," Barrett replied. Was he finally admitting that the name of his ranch and his phone passcode *weren't* coincidences? "She was already named that when I fostered her."

"Do you foster many horses?" she asked.

"When I have the room and the time."

"Don't let him fool you." Manny jerked a thumb toward Barrett. "This one's a sucker for taking in the ugliest, oldest, and saddest looking creatures that nobody else wants. B.D.'s motto should be 'the more flea-bitten, the better.'"

The older neighbor's use of the alias was a reminder of the new life Barrett had built for himself since he'd left Tenacity. But it also confirmed what Nina had thought all along. If this rough-and-tumble ex-cop was willing to vouch for Barrett's character, then that should be enough proof that Barrett was the same person he'd always been.

An engine sounded outside the stables, and the three of them went to the yard to see a big white van with *Royal Flush* painted across the side. Although, by now it was pretty obvious to everyone that whatever was causing the flooded mess was going to require more than a household plumber.

Manny was the first to greet the newcomer, whose triple-extra-large-sized uniform shirt had a logo with five playing cards, then introduced him. "Little Al is one of my poker buddies and said we can use some of his leak-detection equipment to get an idea of where the water's coming from."

Little Al was anything but little, but he moved quickly for a big man.

After about an hour, he took off a pair of what looked to be night-vision goggles and wiped his brow with a green handkerchief. "Looks like one of the tree roots cracked into the main line here."

"But the majority of the water seems to be bubbling up closer to the stables," Barrett said.

"Yep. The original crack has been there awhile and traveled down the main line until it got to here, where the pressure built up enough to cause everything to burst."

"So I need to replace a thirty-foot section of pipe?"

"Yes and no," Little Al said. "The pipe leading to the stables is older than my great-granny. And it's a main line, which means the whole thing will need to come out and be replaced. The good news is that it runs off the well here, unlike your house which is connected to the county water line."

"What's the bad news?" Barrett asked.

"Well, it's gonna be a big project with a lot of digging and heavy machinery. Which means your horses are not going to like the noise or being without water for that long."

Nina didn't blame Barrett for muttering a curse word under his breath. In fact, she had a few more choice words she would've added. With all the work needing to be done and horses to temporarily relocate, there was no way Barrett would be coming back to Tenacity anytime soon.

Chapter Ten

Trenching out over fifty feet of crumbling pipe and installing a new water line was a big issue. Weirdly, though, it was the least overwhelming problem Barrett was currently facing.

Unlike embarking on a fifteen-year-old investigation that was only giving him more questions than answers or figuring out where things stood with his former high school girlfriend (he got more pleasure than he should every time he heard Nina explain that they never actually broke up), the water leak on his property seemed like it would be the easiest thing to repair. Probably because he knew exactly what he was dealing with and exactly which steps he needed to take in order to fix it.

Nina said that they would probably think better once they got some food in their stomachs and offered to drive into town to pick up sandwiches. Which meant Nina was hungry, despite already eating two sausage-and-egg breakfast sandwiches plus his hash browns when he hadn't eaten them quickly enough.

"She didn't ask what I wanted," Manny said as Nina navigated the half mud, half dirt driveway in Barrett's truck.

"Apparently, Nina's superpower is knowing what everyone wants to eat." Barrett chuckled. "And solving cold cases."

"Well, she was pretty good with Big Betty back in the stables and definitely knows her way around a ranch. Horses, food, and crime solving." Manny chuckled. "Sounds like my kind of woman. If she ever decides to make your breakup official, maybe I'll ask her out."

If anyone else—especially Brent Woodson—had said the same thing about Nina, Barrett would've been eaten alive with jealousy. But hearing his older neighbor say it made it easier to laugh off as a joke. "She's too young for you, old man."

"And she's too pretty for a brooding criminal in hiding like you. What's going on with the Tenacity case anyway?"

Barrett updated his neighbor while Little Al put away all his equipment and made a few calls to his contractor friends. But since there weren't many new developments happening in Tenacity, Barrett still had time to call his insurance company and file a claim for the burst pipe.

When Nina returned, she got out of the truck with a cup carrier and grocery-sized bag of food. She set everything on the small table on the front porch and then let herself into the house. Barrett experienced a tug low in his belly that wasn't from hunger pains. It was from wondering if this was how it could be if Nina were in his life as something more than… Ah, hell, he didn't even know what they were, let alone how to define what was going on between them.

When she returned to the patio with a stack of plates, napkins, and silverware, Manny rubbed his hands together and said, "Let's see how she did guessing our orders."

Nina handed Little Al a plastic container holding a giant salad topped with grilled chicken. Al scrunched his nose. "I didn't want a salad."

"I know." Nina smiled sympathetically. "But earlier when you were scanning the garden area with your leak-detection equipment, you said your wife has been on your case about eating healthier and told you to eat more servings of rabbit food—your words, not mine—with every meal. But I also got you some loaded chili-cheese tater tots to go with it because potatoes are vegetables."

"Atta girl." Little Al sat on the porch swing, taking up most of the space.

"Manny, you got the meatball calzone because you kept talking about the pizza from New York and how you can't properly fold the slices you get here in Montana." Nina passed the older man his plate. "This is already folded for you."

Barrett's neighbor shot him a look of surprise and then nodded. "Not bad."

"And for you…" Nina turned to Barrett. "The foot-long pastrami with extra mustard and pickles."

"So close," he told her, pinching his finger and his thumb an inch apart. "I hate pickles."

"I know, but I like them and you're going to end up sharing half your sandwich with me. So I told them to put all your pickles on my side. Plus a large order of fries that I won't touch because I know you're still holding a grudge about me accidentally eating your hash browns this morning."

"I don't think there was anything accidental about it," Barrett said but couldn't stop himself from winking. "That bag doesn't look big enough to hold a cast-iron skillet. So what did you order for yourself?"

Nina stuck out her tongue in his direction, which made him want to carry her inside the house so she could use it for something other than teasing him. But they had company.

Or rather, *he* had company. Although she was playing an amazing role of hostess, and it would be so natural to…

No. He wasn't going to go down that road. Nina's life was in Tenacity. His was here. They weren't playing house.

"I got the Italian melt," she told him. "And if you're nice, I'll let you have a bite."

"You're getting half of my sandwich, yet I only get one bite of yours?"

"Welcome to marriage, kid," Manny said around his mouthful of calzone. "Or in your case, long-term relationships."

"You two aren't married?" Little Al asked.

"No, they've been together for the past fifteen years, though." Manny was sitting on the lone rocking chair, which left Barrett and Nina to sit on the top porch step, their shared food spread out between them.

"Not physically together," Nina explained, but the plumber only looked more confused. "We're just boyfriend and girlfriend."

"It's complicated," Barrett said quickly, still not comfortable sharing his life story with random strangers. "Did you find a contractor who was able to do the work?"

The rest of lunch was spent sitting on the porch discussing the reason why Barrett and Nina were here in the first place—fixing the water issue. Barrett checked his emails on his phone and was relieved to see that Little Al's friend was on the list of approved contractors the insurance adjuster had sent over. The next step was to figure out when the work would start, how long it would last, and where to move the horses.

"I've got room for three more," Manny said. He was currently housing the two horses who'd been displaced by the flooded stalls. "Six more if you don't mind doubling them up."

"I'm sure my brother Julian can take a couple out at his ranch," Nina suggested.

"But that's in Tenacity."

"Is that thing just for show?" Nina pointed to his horse trailer parked outside the barn.

"I wasn't talking about the logistics of getting them there," Barrett replied. "I just meant that this is their home. They're Whitehorn horses."

Nina studied his face, as if she was reading something more into what he was saying. Barrett focused on the remainder of his sandwich because he had a feeling he knew exactly what it was.

"They'll still be Whitehorn horses when they come back." Manny shrugged, then wiped his hands on his jeans as he stood. "But I'll leave it to you guys to figure out. I better get back to my place and get my stable ready for more guests."

Manny drove off, and Little Al said he had another job to look at and would return at four to meet with the contractor.

"We should probably get started cleaning up the flooded stalls," Nina said as she collected the dirty plates. "That straw is going to smell like mildew and wet dog."

Barrett should've offered to take the dishes inside, but he was too grateful for the opportunity to do more demanding physical labor. And for the opportunity to avoid talking about why he'd reacted so strongly to taking his horses to Julian's ranch. Plus, standing at the kitchen sink with Nina would feel too…homey. So he let her continue to play the role of hostess while he got to work.

Thankfully, once Nina met him at the stables, she pulled

a pair of his rubber work boots over her red ones, grabbed a pitchfork, and got right to work beside him.

They moved in harmony, working around each other without having to communicate while they loaded the wheelbarrow with wet straw and swept out inches of standing water. Barrett had some sandbags stored from earlier in the spring, and he placed them outside the double doors to help route the leak away from the stables.

When he returned inside, he found Nina standing outside Big Betty's stall, petting the horse's muzzle and telling her how much she was going to enjoy her visit to Julian's ranch. Betty whinnied, and Nina turned her head to look behind her shoulder at Barrett. "See. I think she wants a little field trip to Tenacity."

"No, she just wants another one of those molasses treats you keep sneaking her every time you think I'm not paying attention," Barrett replied. "Besides, you already have a Big Betty there that, frankly, looks a lot worse than this one."

"Not anymore. The guys from the scrap-metal yard towed her away yesterday. I wouldn't mind having another one."

"Betty's not just a temporary fix, you know." Barrett knew he sounded like a petulant child who didn't want to share his favorite toy. "She gets attached easily."

"Do you want to talk about why you don't want any of your horses going to Tenacity?"

"Not really," he replied honestly. It hadn't felt warm in here when they'd started, but they'd been working nonstop the past couple of hours. He took off his hat to push back his sweat-dampened hair.

"I'm not going to steal your horses, Barrett. I'll even help you bring them back."

"It's not that," he started, then stopped. How could he make someone like her understand?

"Then what is it?" Her touch was whisper soft but comforting as she ran her palm along his bicep.

"You've always lived in the same place, Nina."

"Okay?"

"But I didn't. Not after we left. If I don't count the motels—and there were a lot of them that first year—we lived in five different apartments in five different cities. It wasn't until I started college full-time when I told my parents I wasn't moving with them again and found a room to rent close to the university. It was tiny and crammed with mismatched furniture people left by the side of the road, and the whole place always smelled like tuna casserole even though the oven didn't work. But I stayed there as long as I could stand it because I didn't want to have to move again. And because it was cheap."

"I'm sorry, Barrett. I can only imagine how that must have felt."

"I don't think you can imagine it, Nina. You grew up in the perfect house with the perfect family."

"I assure you that the Sanchezes were not...*are* not perfect."

"I get that. But it was still better than..." Barrett sighed. "I'm not saying I lived in a dump or that my parents didn't take care of me. They were fine. But I always wanted what you guys had. Anyway, when I finally saved up enough money to buy this place, Big Betty came with it. She'd been fostered to different ranches, shuffled from place to place, and the previous owner didn't want to deal with the hassle of transporting her. She hates getting loaded into the trailer the same way I once hated getting loaded into my parents' car every time we moved. I promised her that she wouldn't ever have to leave here."

"I get it." Nina continued rubbing his arm softly. "We don't have to take her away from her home. But what about the other horses?"

"I mean, I didn't exactly make the same commitment to them. And obviously, the colts will eventually leave when they're old enough for me to sell them. It is a horse-breeding ranch after all. But if I can avoid shuffling them around too much, then that's what I'm going to do." Barrett shrugged, causing her hand to slide down to his forearm. She took his hand in hers and squeezed it but didn't say anything. So he asked, "Is this the part where you tell me how silly it is for a grown man to be projecting his childhood insecurities on a bunch of animals who are happy to go wherever there's ample food?"

"It's a bit impractical but not silly." She lifted onto her tiptoes and put both arms around his neck. "But I won't hold it against you. I do impractical things all the time."

The way Nina looked at him in invitation made Barrett want the most impractical thing of all. It had been almost a week since their last kiss, and he doubted that he'd ever get enough of her. Pulling her body closer to his, Nina's lips opened slightly—

A horn blasted outside, and Barrett muttered another curse word as he pulled away from Nina. The only satisfaction from the contractor's interruption was the knowledge that it was getting too late in the day to drive back to Tenacity.

Which meant Nina would likely be staying the night.

Nina's stomach threatened to growl as Barrett and the contractor finally shook hands after agreeing on a price and the schedule for the pipe repairs. It was already seven o'clock in the evening, and her lips were tingling in anticipation of Barrett's almost kiss three hours ago. By the time the contractor drove away, her stomach decided it couldn't stay silent any longer.

"Is that your way of telling me that you want to head into town and get some dinner?" Barrett asked.

"In this?" Nina tugged on her cotton shirt, which smelled like mildewed straw and had dried stiffly after she'd sweated through it earlier.

His hands followed hers, and his thumbs traced along the line of buttons between her breasts. "I think you look great. But if you want to take a shower and put on something different, then be my guest."

She took a step closer to him. "What if I wanted to take a shower and not put on anything at all?"

"Then you can still be my guest." With that, Barrett kissed her again.

His fingers made quick work of her buttons, and his hands slid over the satin fabric of her bra to cover each of her breasts. She arched her back, allowing him full access, which he took.

Nina was breathless and practically panting when she pulled away long enough to say, "I hope you didn't leave the condoms back at the Tenacity Inn."

"I've had one in my wallet since last Sunday." His finger traced under the lace trim of her bra. "Just in case."

"So then who gets to shower first?"

"Since you have no problem sharing my food…" The corner of his lips turned up in a satisfied grin, and before she knew it, his arms were around her, his hands cupping her rear as he effortlessly lifted her until her legs had no choice but to wrap around his waist. "Then you shouldn't mind sharing my shower."

Barrett carried her across the yard and up the porch

steps, not the slightest bit distracted by Nina's mouth on his. It wasn't until they got to the front door that Nina yelped in slight protest.

"What's wrong?" he asked.

"Our boots are filthy. We should probably take them off and throw our clothes in the wash."

"Nina Sanchez, I have been waiting fifteen years to haul you to my bed. You're lucky I'm willing to make a detour to the shower."

When Barrett kicked the front door closed behind them, Nina had never felt more lucky in her life. In all the different ways she'd imagined her first time making love to Barrett Deroy, she had never thought of it happening in the shower.

They helped each other undress and then took advantage of the hot spray of water and slipperiness of the soap as they explored each other's naked bodies. "I can't take it anymore," Barrett groaned, reaching behind her to shut off the faucet. "I need to be inside of you."

"Then what are you waiting for?" Nina asked.

This time, when he lifted her up to carry her out of the shower, there were no clothes, no barrier to prevent the tip of his erection from sliding along her damp skin. Nina gasped, rocking her hips against him until his shaft was perfectly positioned. Barrett groaned before setting her down on the edge of the bathroom counter. She thought her overeager movements had caused him to lose his grip on her, but then she realized he had reached into the pocket of his discarded jeans and was rolling on the condom.

Standing between her open thighs, Barrett said, "We'll make it to the bed next time."

When he entered her, a ragged moan tore from the back of Nina's throat. He immediately stiffened. "Are you okay?"

"I'm better than okay." She wrapped her calves around his waist to pull him in deeper. "Please don't stop now."

And he didn't.

The sun was setting, and their clothes and boots were still in a pile on the bathroom floor. But at least Barrett had managed to get Nina into his bed. Or rather on top of it.

"Are you cold?" he asked, his finger making a slow circle on her lower back.

"Maybe a little." She smiled up at him. "My host didn't offer me so much as a towel when I got out of the shower."

Barrett chuckled. "He must not be very accustomed to having guests. Which is why you won't be surprised to find out that he isn't exactly prepared to make you a proper meal either."

"That's a shame." She wrapped her hand around the back of his neck and pulled his head closer to hers. "Because now that I know what I've been missing out on all these years, it's going to be a long night making up for lost time. We'll definitely need some sustenance."

The second time they made love, it was slower and they took their time learning each other's bodies. Afterward, Nina insisted that she really did need to eat and helped herself to one of the T-shirts hanging in Barrett's closet.

She had looked good in his bed, but she looked even more amazing in his kitchen, opening and closing cupboards and taking inventory of his empty fridge and over-stocked freezer. Hope blossomed in his chest, even as he tried to unsuccessfully put his expectations in check. He couldn't help it. Nina just looked good in his life.

After a few moments, though, he realized that they were both standing there and food wasn't miraculously appearing.

"Sorry about the lack of fresh ingredients," he said. "I

didn't go to the store because I wasn't sure how long I'd be in Tenacity. I've got some frozen dinners we can put in the oven. Or we could thaw some steaks, but I don't know what we'd have for side dishes."

"I have a small confession," she said, staring at his stove instead of him. "And it may change how you feel about me."

He came up behind her and slipped his arms around her waist. "Were you the one who took the money and hid it out on Juniper Road?"

He'd meant the words to be a joke, but he could feel a slight tensing in Nina's muscles. "No, but thanks for the timely reminder about the dark cloud still hanging over our heads."

"The cloud doesn't seem that dark anymore." He kissed her neck. "So let's forget about it for a while longer. Or at least for as long as we're in Whitehorn. We can think about it when we return to Tenacity. Now, please tell me your confession."

She sighed and leaned back against his chest. "I can't cook."

"Oh, I wasn't expecting you to be some sort of accomplished chef or anything. I'm pretty basic when it comes to cooking anyway."

"No, like I mean I ruin everything I try to make. My mom tried to teach me, but the best I can do is frozen waffles and ramen noodles. The kind already in a cup." Nina turned to face him. "You made that comment the other day about how you used to love coming to our house because my mom was such a good cook and you grew up on ready-made meals, and now seems like as good of time as any to tell you to lower those expectations."

"Nina, when it comes to you, I don't have any expectations. I'm not looking for a wife or for someone to take care of me. I've been on my own for a while now." He was trying to reassure her, but her normally expressive face seemed rather blank. She must've been exhausted. "I don't want to brag or anything, but I even have my own cast-iron skillet."

There. That got a small smile from her. He steered her toward a chair at the small kitchen table and found a boxed pancake mix that only required water.

"You're always taking care of everyone else. Let me take care of you."

Chapter Eleven

When Nina woke up in his bed Saturday morning, Barrett suggested going into town for breakfast. She was relieved to have something to do, somewhere to go so that the awkward conversation that had happened in his kitchen last night didn't happen again.

She didn't want to think about how things between them were just temporary while they were here in his world. Soon, they'd have to go back to Tenacity where things might've been improving but would never feel like home for Barrett the way Whitehorn clearly did.

Not that she could blame the man for being so much more at ease here. Nina shouldn't have been surprised, but the people in Whitehorn who knew Barrett—or B.D., as they called him—seemed to genuinely like him. Several people waved at them as they drove past. Nobody refused to serve him at the diner. They even ran into another rancher at the hardware store who'd heard about the problem on the Double N and offered to house a few of Barrett's horses.

Each friendly interaction reinforced Nina's belief that Barrett was still a good person, a trustworthy person. Unfortunately, it also reinforced her loved ones' predictions that he was going to break her heart again by leaving.

Not that they were even at the stage in their relationship

where she should've been thinking about things like long-term commitments and the possibility of eventually living together. But it was clear that Barrett's heart belonged in Whitehorn. Which meant that if Nina wanted to be with him, she would have to leave her own heart in Tenacity.

"When do you need to get back?" Barrett asked as they left the hardware store. She did a double take as though he'd just read her thoughts. But instead of responding, she stared at him blankly. He tilted his head in confusion and repeated the question adding, "I'm assuming you need to go back to work on Monday?"

"Oh." She shook her head as the outside sounds of the main street filtered into her brain. "Yes, I need to be back in Tenacity by Monday morning."

"In that case, you wouldn't mind staying one more night to help me out?"

It wasn't the most romantic invitation, but it wasn't like they'd come to his ranch on a carefree holiday. Not knowing what to expect, Nina hadn't packed a suitcase, but luckily she'd thrown a change of clothes and some toiletries into a tote bag before he'd picked her up yesterday morning. "As long as we can stop by the grocery store first."

"You read my mind." He put his arm around her shoulders and kissed her on the lips, right there in the parking lot at the hardware store where anyone passing by could see them. That had to mean he cared about her, right? This was his town, and he was all but advertising that she was someone he cared about. "Plus, my mom should be working this morning, and we can get that over with."

Nina didn't love the way Barrett had phrased that. Was he worried about how his mom would react to seeing her? While her family hadn't exactly thrown a parade to welcome him back into their fold, it was because he was the one who'd left with no explanation. As far as the Deroys should've been concerned, Nina didn't owe them an explanation about anything. So maybe Barrett was worried that Nina would overwhelm his mom with questions or bring back memories that the woman didn't want to think about. He had said that his parents hadn't wanted him to go to Tenacity, even if it meant clearing his name.

It turned out that Nina's overthinking was for nothing because when they got to the store, the manager told Barrett that his mom had called off work that day. Then the manager asked, "Has your mom met your new girlfriend yet?"

"Technically, she's my old girlfriend," Barrett told the middle-aged woman, causing her pencil-drawn eyebrows to lift. He took Nina's hand, which caused the eyebrows to go even higher. "I'll give my mom a call later to check on her."

Barrett casually strode toward a row of shopping carts, ignoring the people at the registers who were staring at them. Nina had to tug on his arm to get his attention. She whispered out the side of her mouth. "I think you just confused your mom's boss."

"How?" Barrett released her hand to choose a cart.

"You told her I'm your old girlfriend."

"That's how you explained it to Manny."

"No, I just told him that we'd never broken up," Nina clarified.

"Which would make you my current girlfriend."

"Except you didn't say *current*. You said *old*."

"Well, the manager can clearly see that you're not old."

"Barrett, *old girlfriend* means *ex-girlfriend*."

"No, it doesn't." He stopped at the deli counter. "Should we get stuff to make sandwiches? We can't screw those up too badly."

But Nina was still full from breakfast and wasn't going

to let him distract her with the promise of more food. "Look, I get it that you don't want to get involved in a relationship right now, and just because we slept together doesn't mean I'm going to get the wrong idea or try to lock you down."

"I appreciate that." He slipped his arm around her waist and kissed her lightly. "So then why are we talking about defining things? Ex-girlfriend, old girlfriend, current girlfriend. It shouldn't matter."

"I agree. But when you say *that*—" she jerked her thumb toward the area where they'd had the conversation with the manager, then pointed at his hand, which was settled on the most intimate part of her hip "—and then do this, it confuses people."

"Well, people shouldn't be asking me personal questions." In his defense, he had warned Nina before that he liked keeping a low profile. Just because he was settled into Whitehorn and intended to stay here indefinitely didn't mean he was any more comfortable with the same small-town gossip that he complained about in Tenacity.

Nina used to think she was so good at reading people, but Barrett Deroy, the person she once thought she knew better than anyone else, went from closed book to open book to comic book at times. She didn't even know which page she was on, so all she could do was try to enjoy the story.

When he told the clerk behind the counter how much deli meat he wanted, Nina told the man to double it. They didn't intend to buy too many groceries, since the plan was to return to Tenacity on Sunday. But for every item Barrett put in the cart, she added three more things.

When they returned to his ranch, she put away the groceries and made them sandwiches while he loaded six horses onto his trailer. Nina heard several crashing sounds and was in such a hurry to get into the yard, she didn't realize she'd brought half the head of lettuce she'd been slicing with her.

"Is everything okay?" she asked Barrett when she saw him shutting the back of the horse trailer.

"Betty is trying to get out of her stall," he explained. "The more I stand there trying to calm her down, the more unreasonable she gets."

"Maybe she wants to go with us," Nina suggested.

"No. She hates the trailer. She must sense it's outside, and it's making her nervous."

"Should I stay with her?" Nina asked, not waiting for an answer as she walked into the stables to soothe the poor horse who was stomping around her stall and neighing loudly. Betty paused, watching her approach, then put her head over the top railing and sniffed in the direction of the lettuce. Nina offered a small leaf to the horse, who took it quickly and seemed to calm down.

Betty whinnied again when the truck engine started, but Nina remained there, stroking the horse's muzzle and telling her what a good, brave girl she was being. "Are you having separation anxiety? It's nothing to be ashamed of. My dad has a goat with separation anxiety and does the exact same thing every time he has to leave in the mornings."

Nina heard the truck pull away and thought Barrett had left without her. But a few minutes went by, and she saw him standing by the stable doors. "I parked down the driveway so she wouldn't see the trailer. How's she doing?"

"I think she's okay now."

"The boys I had working on the ranch while I was gone said she'd been a drama queen. I thought they were just exaggerating."

They decided that it would be best for Barrett to stay with the horse while Nina packed their sandwiches to go. When they were sure that Big Betty was finally calm, they walked down to where Barrett had left the truck and trailer and drove the five miles to drop off some of his horses at the ranch of the friend they'd met in town.

On their way home, Barrett pulled the truck into a clearing and pulled out the sandwiches. They sat on the tailgate, having a picnic lunch while enjoying an incredible view of the mountain range in the distance.

Once they got back, another neighbor arrived with a horse trailer and loaded several more horses to take temporarily. Again, Nina stayed with Betty, who gave Barrett a side-eye while more of her stablemates left.

Later that afternoon, Barrett rode Big Betty and Nina rode one of the thoroughbreds over to Manny's ranch. Nina was leading another horse behind her, while Barrett had the reins of two more. But as they approached the stables of the Bar None, Betty suddenly stopped and refused to take another step. Manny laughed at the mare's stubbornness and helped Nina lead the other horses into the stalls where they'd be staying temporarily.

Originally, Manny was going to drive them back to the Double N, but when it became more and more apparent that Big Betty wasn't going to be convinced, Barrett said, "Let's just take her back and try again tomorrow morning."

Nina climbed into the saddle behind Barrett, but the draft horse didn't seem to mind the extra weight. In fact, she nearly galloped home as though the only place she wanted to be was in her stall.

That night, they were too exhausted to do much more than enjoy the rotisserie chicken they'd picked up at the store along with a small cheese-and-fruit tray and a bottle of wine. They made love again, and before Nina fell asleep in Barrett's arms, she thought that maybe she could make a home for herself in Whitehorn.

"I'm starting to think that it might be best if I let her stay here," Barrett said the following morning when they went out to the stables to feed Big Betty. The horse ignored him for several minutes and even refused to eat the feed he'd just scooped into her trough. It was almost as though she was punishing him for abandoning her in the stables all by herself. "I can put her in one of the corrals so she can watch the construction going on."

"I don't know…" Nina scanned the empty stalls around them. "If we leave and she's the only horse here, she might go stir crazy."

Barrett couldn't believe he was allowing his schedule to be dictated by the stubborn demands of a horse with separation anxiety. "I'm going to get you one apple," he told Betty. "Just one. And then Nina and I are going to load the truck and be gone for another week. Manny will come check on you, and you'll have the whole corral to yourself. You probably won't like the tractors, but maybe someone on the construction crew will have some carrot sticks in their lunch that they want to get rid of."

Nina was smiling at him as he spoke.

"Are you going to make fun of me for trying to negotiate with a horse?"

"Never," Nina replied, a sparkle in her brown eyes. "Besides, I'm sure she believes you. Or at least she wants you to think she does so you'll give her another apple."

It turned out Nina was right. She was walking to the truck with her small overnight bag just as Barrett was leading Betty to the outside corral. The mare stopped as soon as she saw Nina and would not budge. In fact, the horse nearly pulled the reins out of Barrett's hand as she jerked her head and sidestepped toward the truck.

"You're not going with us," Barrett tried to explain, but Betty wasn't having it. He decided to try a different approach. "Nina, will you back up the truck toward the trailer hitch? If she thinks we're going to load her into the trailer, then she will go straight to the corral."

"Barrett Deroy," Nina tried to chastise him, but a giggle slipped out. "I've seen a lot of things over the years as a horse trainer, but I've yet to see reverse psychology work."

Nina moved the truck, but instead of having the desired effect, Big Betty did something she'd never done before. She tugged Barrett toward the trailer.

Nina smiled again. "I'm telling you she wants to go with us."

"They don't allow horses at the Tenacity Inn," Barrett tried to explain to the mare who was now using its front hoof to paw at the trailer door.

"Did I tell you about Noodles, my dad's goat?"

"Your dad has a goat named Noodles?" Barrett asked, wishing he'd had another cup of coffee.

"It hates leaving the farm, but it wants to go everywhere my dad goes. One of the neighbor's chickens had to come spend the night in the small barn with Noodles when my parents went to Bronco to visit Marisa."

"So you think I should get a chicken companion for Big Betty?"

Nina shook her head. "No, that'd be silly. Nobody would want to loan you a chicken for the entire week."

"Then where are you going with this whole story?" He knew there must be some sort of underlying plan because Nina rarely did anything without a good reason. But he was too frustrated with his contrary horse to understand whatever she was trying to explain.

"Well, *we*—" Nina undid the latch that opened the trailer door, and Betty immediately walked inside "—are apparently going to Tenacity to take Betty to meet Noodles."

After several trips between the stables and the trailer to load up everything Big Betty would need to spend a week in Tenacity, and several text messages between Nina and her dad to make sure the small barn would be able to accommodate a two-thousand-pound horse with separation anxiety, Barrett was back on the highway heading toward the town he'd wanted to leave behind.

Not that he'd wanted to leave Nina behind. It was just that he'd felt so much more relaxed, so much more at ease since they'd been in Whitehorn. He'd almost been tempted to ask Nina if she would ever think about the possibility of relocating.

However, he was steadfast in his determination to not get too far ahead of things by getting into a relationship before he found out who'd been the one behind the missing money.

"Oh wow," Nina said once they were on the highway. "My mom just texted and asked if you want to come for dinner tonight."

"You sound shocked."

"Not shocked," Nina said unconvincingly. "I knew she would come around eventually."

Eventually? That didn't convey the promise that Barrett would be getting the warmest welcome from the Sanchezes. In fact, it almost made it sound like they were resigned and giving into their daughter's wishes. Much like he'd just given into Big Betty.

"What time is dinner?" He looked in his review mirror.

"Betty isn't the best traveler, and we might need to make a few stops if she starts getting restless back there."

Nina fired off a message, and a few moments later her phone pinged with a response. "My mom said to keep her updated on our progress and she'll put…uh…stuff…in the oven when we're getting close."

Okay, so they were willing to hold dinner for him. That had to be a good thing, right? Except Barrett had heard the hesitation in Nina's voice.

"What stuff?"

"Hmmm?" Nina murmured as she kept her face averted to stare intently at the flat fields outside the passenger-side window.

"What is your mom putting in the oven, Nina?"

She sighed, then turned to face him. "Enchiladas suizas."

He would've laughed if he wasn't already on edge about showing up on their doorstep with a horse that needed to be babysat by their goat. "So it's a test?"

"I'm sure it's not a test." Nina rolled her bottom lip between her teeth, as though she could hold back her smile. "She probably forgot how much you hated her version of it."

"I didn't hate it," Barrett insisted. "I just thought it was better at Castillo's."

"Well then, when you eat my mom's, pretend that you like it more than Pablo Castillo's."

"For all I know, I might," he said, trying to stay optimistic.

Several hours later, the only thing he was optimistic about was that Mrs. Sanchez was believing his lie.

"It's the best enchiladas suizas I've ever had," Barrett said as five sets of eyes watched him swallow his first bite. "Have you always used this much sour cream?"

"Yes." Nicole Sanchez nodded. "Do you think it's too much?"

"Nope." Barrett shook his head and loaded another forkful. "It tastes like the perfect amount to me."

He must have successfully convinced the rest of the Sanchezes because the tension suddenly lightened and the mood turned friendlier. Diego and Julian and their fiancées were there, along with their children.

Mr. Sanchez asked him about his ranch, but thankfully, nobody brought up why Barrett and his family had left fifteen years ago. At least they didn't until Luca arrived. His mom scolded her youngest son for being late, but he quickly filled his plate and grabbed an empty seat between Jenna and Ruby.

The first thing Luca said to Barrett was "So were the Deroys as surprised to see Nina in Whitehorn as we were to see you here in Tenacity?"

"Actually, we didn't see my parents while we were there."

"Really? They always seemed to like Nina just fine before." Luca took a long drink of his iced tea. "You'd think they'd want to offer any support they could to the woman who has been working tirelessly all these years to vindicate their son."

"Take it down a notch, Luca," Nina warned her brother.

But Barrett didn't need her protecting him. "They had to go out of town unexpectedly."

"Again?" Luca lifted his dark eyebrows a bit too high, as though he wasn't all that surprised. "That's quite a habit for some of the Deroys."

This time, Mrs. Sanchez spoke up. "You're being rude to our guest, Luca."

"How's the investigation going anyway?" Diego asked, redirecting the topic.

"It's going okay, I guess." Nina looked at Barrett for assurance. He gave her a nod, and she filled in her family of what they'd found out so far, which was mostly just speculation.

Even to Barrett, who knew he hadn't done anything wrong, the circumstantial evidence hadn't exactly redeemed him, let alone proved his innocence. He couldn't blame the Sanchezes for doubting him. If Nina was *his* daughter or sister, he'd also be telling her to run from trouble and not look back.

Will Sanchez wiped his mouth and put his napkin on his empty plate. "I wonder why the Woodsons were so intent on blaming you, Barrett."

"Well, sir, Brent and I never really got along. He was always jealous of my position on the team and my relationship with your daughter."

"And what exactly is your relationship with my daughter?"

"Dad…" Nina's tone gave a slight warning.

"No, *mija*." Her father held up a work-roughened hand. "Barrett doesn't mind answering my questions, do you?"

"Of course I don't, sir." Barrett sat up straighter. "But the truth of the matter is that—"

"It's none of anyone's business," Nina said, cutting him off. "I'm thirty years old, and I'm responsible for my own decisions, including who I'm dating."

"So you *are* dating," Julian confirmed as though it was some big revelation.

Ruby, Julian's fiancée who worked at the inn and probably knew that Nina had been seen leaving his room, was apparently keeping her lips sealed.

"Mr. Sanchez, I want to assure you that I have always had the best intentions where your daughter is concerned. When I stayed away for so long, it was because I thought I was protecting her from all the gossip and speculation. Even now, I'm still trying to protect her from all the drama my return has caused—not that I've done a good job of that."

"Not that she's letting you— Ow!" Luca glared at his sister across the table from him. "Why did you kick me?"

Before the siblings could turn the conversation into a petty squabble, Barrett continued speaking to their father. "I'll tell you the same thing I told Nina. My number one priority in Tenacity is clearing my name."

Luca held up two fingers at Nina. "That makes you his second priority."

Nina threw a crumpled napkin at her brother's head.

"Knock it off, you two." Mrs. Sanchez had mastered the fine art of scolding her children in a quiet but firm voice.

Barrett put his arm around the back of Nina's chair. "Nobody is my second priority. I'm saying that I have to resolve some things before I can give Nina the commitment she deserves."

"Jeez." Luca rolled his eyes. "You're a smooth talker, just like your old—"

Nina's brother stopped speaking mid-sentence, and everyone at the table stared at him expectantly. The awkward pause was short-lived as a baby cried, followed by Diego and Mrs. Sanchez both racing to be the first one to pick up almost-one-year-old Robbie from the portable crib where she'd fallen asleep. Conversations quickly resumed around the table as if the awkwardness was no longer hanging in the air. Jenna and Ruby spoke about the lack of wedding venues in Tenacity, Mr. Sanchez and Luca spoke about the latest hay crop, Julian went to check on baby Jay, who wasn't disturbed by his future cousin's crying, and Ruby's four-year-old daughter, Emery, asked Nina if they could go check on how Big Betty was getting along with Noodles the goat.

Barrett had never been so relieved to excuse himself from a table. He stacked the plates closest to him to carry them toward the kitchen, when it suddenly got quiet again. He turned to the table and saw everyone's eyes on him. Again.

"What are you doing, Barrett?" Diego asked, returning to the room empty-handed. Apparently, his mother, who was walking behind him cuddling Robbie, had beat him in the race to get to her.

"I'm going to start the dishes," Barrett replied as though it was the most natural thing in the world. But maybe the Sanchez family rules had changed since he'd been gone. "I thought the boys do kitchen cleanup on Sundays?"

"It's been a while since Mom and Dad enforced that one." Julian also had a baby in his arms now. "Unfortunately, I can't help since I'm holding Jay."

"I do my own dishes in the bunkhouse all week long," Luca started to complain, but his father gave him what the Sanchez boys referred to as "the look."

"Oh, your life must be so rough, Luca." Diego laughed. "You have to clean up after just yourself."

"Don't act like you were eager to start scrubbing pots and pans, D," Luca told his brother. "I saw you hip check your own mom trying to get Robbie so you had an excuse not to help either."

"Did you see Mom land a sharp elbow to my rib cage?" Diego dramatically winced as he stretched to lift the empty serving dish.

"I'll help," Ruby offered.

"No," Mrs. Sanchez said to her future daughter-in-law. "Barrett is right. It's Sunday, so the boys will take care of the kitchen."

Luca, who was now collecting empty glasses, muttered, "Thanks a lot, Deroy."

Barrett wished he would've gone with Nina and Emery to the barn, but being in the Sanchez home had caused his old instincts to kick in. Once the sink was filling with warm soapy water, he apologized to Luca.

"To be honest, man…" Luca picked up a dish cloth as they settled into their once-familiar routine of Barrett washing and Luca drying. "I needed a break from out there and the whole *big happy family* routine."

"What do you mean?" Barrett asked his old friend.

"Everyone in my family is getting married, getting engaged, having kids, settling down. It's only a matter of time before my parents turn to me and want to know what's taking so long."

"Really?" Barrett passed him a wet plate. "Because, technically, Nina's still single, and I got the impression they weren't exactly excited for her to get involved in a relationship."

"First of all," Luca said, "nobody gives Nina a hard time about anything. You of all people should know that it's pointless to argue with her when her mind is made up. Second of all, of course they're going to be wary about her getting involved in a relationship with the guy who once broke her heart."

"Fair enough." Barrett passed him another plate. Nina was strong-willed, and he had a feeling that if her parents didn't approve of her seeing him, she wouldn't let that stop her. Which was all the more reason why he shouldn't let things get too far between them. He would never want her to have to choose between him and her family.

He was so lost in thought, he hadn't realized Luca was staring at him waiting for the next clean dish to dry. Barrett cleared his throat. "It sounds like Diego and Julian were both still single when they were our age. Did your parents give them a hard time?"

"No," Julian said as he came into the kitchen, balancing Jay on his shoulder. "And nobody is giving Luca a hard time either. If he's not feeling fulfilled in life, that's on him. Our parents just want us to be happy."

"I'd be a lot happier if you were the one doing dishes," Luca said.

"We can switch if you want," Julian said. "I was just looking for Jay's diaper bag since he needs to be changed."

Luca sniffed, then shook his head. "Nope. I can smell that from here."

"What about you, Deroy?" Julian asked.

"I've never even held a baby," Barrett said, using the scrub brush on a stubborn bit of melted cheese stuck to a plate.

"You're missing out." Julian lifted a colorful bag from the rack of hooks by the back door. "Not on the dirty-diaper part, but just on kids in general."

Luca nudged Barrett and whispered, "See what I mean? All of a sudden, nobody's allowed to be happily single around here."

Barrett had lived by himself for so long, it was hard to know if he'd been happy being single or if he just hadn't known anything else. However, being back here with the Sanchezes, plus the recent additions to their family, he began to wonder if it wasn't only Nina he'd been missing all those years. Not that her siblings had completely let their guards down around him. It was obvious that they were still minding what they said in front of him. In fact, Barrett wanted to ask Luca what he'd been about to say when he'd paused mid-sentence at the dining room table earlier. But before he could, Diego returned with several more plates stacked on top of a wooden salad bowl. "Anyone know what's for dessert?"

Barrett doubted it would be strawberry cake, but a guy could dream.

Chapter Twelve

Nina had wanted to go back to the inn with Barrett after dinner on Sunday, but she'd also promised to keep an eye on Big Betty and Noodles. A promise that felt rather pointless on Monday morning when she went to her parents' barn only to be ignored by the horse and goat who'd quickly become the best of pals.

She took a picture of the animals and sent it to Barrett before leaving for work. He replied with a simple thumbs-up emoji, and Nina tried not to read too much into it. While her family hadn't exactly embraced Barrett last night at dinner, they also hadn't been too distant or rude. It was progress, she told herself as she drove to Forrester Farms to remind Gladiator of what they'd been working on before the weekend.

Normally, she wasn't insecure when it came to men or whether they were interested in her. But Barrett was proving more difficult to understand. The physical attraction had added another layer of complexity to a relationship that had once been so easy and effortless. It was as though his head was telling her—and her family last night at dinner—that he didn't want anything serious right now. But his body was telling her something else.

She had just brought Gladiator back to his stall when she got a text from Barrett.

Talked to Marshall and Stanley. Not sure if there are any new developments, but we're meeting at Marshall's office after football practice if you're available. Your uncle said he's bringing over BBQ from a place called Lulu's in Bronco.

Nina gave the stallion a carrot as his reward for doing so well today, then replied, BBQ and investigative work in the same evening? You really know the way to this girl's heart.

Her phone beeped a few minutes later. His text put her earlier insecurity to rest and a smile on her face.

If you stop off at your parents' barn to check on Big Betty and Noodles, let my horse know that you won't be back until morning.

Two hours later, they were sitting in Marshall's conference room, which was really just an extra area behind the reception desk with a long folding table and some mismatched chairs, eating the most delicious pulled pork Nina had ever tasted.

"I ordered some new office furniture, but it got lost somewhere between Chicago and Bozeman," Marshall said around a bite of potato salad.

Nina reached to try that side dish next.

"I think it looks great just like this." Uncle Stanley uncapped a dry-erase marker. Her great-uncle was a simple, no-frills sort of man when it came to his surroundings. However, when it came to dramatic announcements, both he and Winona were the opposite of simple. Not that Winona was overly dramatic when she made her psychic predictions. She was actually very matter-of-fact with her statements. It was what the statements revealed that made things seem so grand.

Uncle Stanley drew a rock and a dollar sign on the white board propped up on an easel. Then he drew a line and wrote the name *Brent Woodson*. "Initially, my bet would've been on this kid stealing the money. I was able to get a log of people going into town hall that day, and even though he never officially signed in, both of his parents worked there and would have had access to the cash. Brent arguably had the biggest motive to frame Barrett. Plus, the money was found out on his dad's old property."

"That was the first person I thought of, too," Marshall said. "In fact, I took things one step further. If the mayor knew his son stole the money, it may be why he was so insistent on pinning the blame on someone else yet also reluctant for a full investigation."

"So we think it was Brent Woodson." Barrett nodded, and Nina realized he had barely touched his food.

"Except we already established that Brent was away at a football camp that week. Besides, why would Brent have gone through all the trouble to steal the money, hide it out on his property, and then never go back for it?" Nina asked. "Especially considering the fact that he was one of the few kids at Tenacity High that didn't get a part time job during the summers because his dad wanted him to focus on football."

"Did his parents give him an allowance?" Marshall asked.

"Not that big of one. Besides, his dad was pretty controlling with the finances," Nina explained. "Barrett, remember that time we were working at the snack bar during Little League and Mrs. Woodson didn't have any cash?"

"I don't think I ever worked the snack bar." Barrett tilted his head. "I always played baseball."

"I was working there, and you came to visit me between games. Mrs. Woodson wanted to buy Brent some sunflower seeds. She asked if we took credit cards. Your dad was there and offered to pay."

"Now I remember," Barrett said. "I had asked him earlier to buy me some gum, and he told me that money didn't grow on trees. But suddenly he was offering to pay for sunflower seeds for the mayor's son."

"He made a comment to Mrs. Woodson about Cliff keeping her on a tight leash, and I always thought it was a weird thing to say because it reminded me of a dog. But then a few years later, my mom took me and Marisa to the beauty shop to get our hair cut, and Mrs. Woodson was sitting there with her hair all done. The mayor came into the shop and paid for her, and then they left together."

"So you think the Woodsons were having money problems?" Uncle Stanley asked. "They did downsize to a smaller property when they left their place on Juniper Road."

"Maybe it was the mayor himself who stole the money." Marshall had moved on to the ribs.

"It also explains why he would be so quick to throw the blame on me yet not launch a full investigation."

How was Barrett not digging into the amazing food spread out before him? It was all Nina could do to pay attention to the names and lines on Uncle Stanley's flowchart. Of course, she'd also been working this case since she was in high school, so she'd already been through every angle she could think of. In fact, she probably had this same exact flowchart on a spiral notebook somewhere in her room.

"I met Mayor Woodson a few days ago," Marshall said.

"I guess I should say the former mayor. He stopped by here to welcome me to town."

"He is pretty friendly," Uncle Stanley said. "Maybe a little too friendly for my tastes."

"Uncle Stanley," Nina said. "You're one to talk. You make friends with people everywhere you go."

"Except I make friends because I'm genuinely interested in having conversations with people and getting to know them. It's what makes me such a good private investigator."

Nina was tempted to remind her uncle that he wasn't an actual P.I. for hire. But unlike Luca, she didn't go around telling people that they should get a real hobby instead of trying to play detective.

"You don't think Cliff Woodson was interested in getting to know Marshall?" Barrett asked.

"Oh, he was definitely interested in getting to know me," Marshall said. "But Mr. Sanchez is right. It wasn't like he was dropping off a welcome basket or asking if I needed anything. In fact, I actually could have used some help when he walked in. I was on the floor trying to assemble a bookshelf, and he didn't even offer to hand me a screwdriver."

"Woodson doesn't look like the type who would put together his own furniture." Uncle Stanley made a tsking sound. "But that's what I mean. He's friendly, but he's not actually trying to be a friend, you know?"

"Exactly." Marshall pointed a half-eaten rib bone at Stanley. "The man was smooth enough not to make it seem like an interrogation. But I still got the vibe that he was sizing me up. He didn't come right out and ask if I was working with Barrett, probably because he's smart enough to know how attorney-client privilege works. Yet there was no doubt that he already knew about our breakfast meeting at the Silver Spur."

"So you think he may have been fishing for information?" Barrett asked.

"To be fair," Nina said, "that's what the four of us have been doing for over a week now. Fishing for information, listening for gossip, and taking hints from anyone and everyone."

"Except we have an interest in solving a case," Uncle Stanley said. "We're trying to figure out who framed Barrett. If Woodson was so interested in finding the missing money, he would've done it a long time ago."

"It's almost as though he doesn't want the case to be solved." Finally, Barrett picked up his fork. "Which would mean that he was somehow involved."

"I'm not saying you're wrong." Nina licked barbecue sauce from her finger. "I've watched enough detective shows to know better than ruling someone out as a suspect. But why blame it on a teenage boy? Especially one as well liked as Barrett."

"Jealousy?" Marshall asked. "If Barrett was well liked, maybe the mayor didn't want anyone rivaling his son."

Nina pondered it for a second. "There was that one case where the mom of a cheerleader plotted against the girl who beat out her daughter as team captain. I suppose that could have been the mayor's motive. But it wasn't like Brent was unpopular."

"True, but Brent was also a senior and it would've been his last year to start as quarterback. Instead, everyone was expecting the coach to pick me."

"That's a tough pill for a father to swallow," Uncle Stanley said. "Especially if they're really into a particular sport.

It's a wonder the mayor didn't accuse the coach of stealing the money to get *him* out of the picture."

"Wait." Nina gulped down the food she was chewing. "Are we seriously thinking that the mayor was behind the money going missing?"

"He had access to it," Barrett said.

"He also had the most to lose," Nina replied. "Clearly, whoever stole the money didn't need it, because they never went back for it."

"Unless the person who stole it *couldn't* come back for it."

"Like they died?" Uncle Stanley asked.

Barrett raised his hand. "Or they went missing for fifteen years."

"Well, we already ruled out that it wasn't you," Nina said. "So if it was someone else who went missing or died, then we'd be wrong in assuming that it was the mayor. And like I said, since the Woodsons weren't hurting for cash, it wouldn't have been worth it for the mayor. As much as the man loves his son being a football star, he loves the town of Tenacity even more. That renovation fund was supposed to be Mayor Woodson's legacy. He spent years trying to work out a deal to get more businesses to move here."

"Maybe we're barking up the wrong tree with the Woodsons," Marshall suggested. "That money was supposed to fund the revitalization of the Tenacity Trail and finance a dinosaur dig that could have put the town on the map. I heard that when the money disappeared, the folks behind the restoration decided to take their organization elsewhere. Maybe the person who stole the money didn't want the dinosaur dig to come to town."

Uncle Stanley scratched his chin, leaving a smear of barbecue sauce. "Who would benefit from keeping the dinosaur dig from happening? Or improving the Tenacity Trail? Not another business owner, since they should want to increase tourism and potential revenue."

"I already looked into that angle several years ago," Nina said. "I researched whether there was a rival dinosaur park or if the people behind the renovation fund had any enemies or anyone who would want to see them fail."

"Did you find anything?" Marshall asked.

"I found an ex-wife of one of the financial backers and a former colleague of one of the paleontologists who might've had an axe to grind. But neither of those leads showed much promise."

"What about competing businesses here in town?" Marshall asked. "I noticed there are two feed stores that seem to manage okay here. But back then was there any business that would've gone under if more competition came to town?"

Okay, so that was something Nina had never thought to look into. She admitted as much to the group. "Let me put together a list of business that were in operation back then."

"I'm already on it." Uncle Stanley pulled a small spiral notepad out of his front shirt pocket. It was the same kind that a detective on TV would've used, and Nina had to hold back a giggle. He was really taking on his new role seriously.

"That's some old-school method of note-taking, Uncle Stanley. I thought you were trying to be more high tech." She nodded toward his open laptop.

"I am. But I can't keep track of all my passwords, and each city and county uses different databases with different log in requirements. I have to write them down." Uncle Stanley used a single finger to hunt and peck on the keyboard as he looked back and forth between his notepad and the computer. "Okay, I'm in."

"We're not hacking into anything, are we?" Barrett asked, concern evident in his eyes. "Because I'm trying to avoid drawing the attention of law enforcement."

"No, this is a public website." Uncle Stanley turned the screen toward them. "Here is a list of everyone who applied for a business license around the time the money went missing. These records have been obtained completely legally."

That was right—Uncle Stanley had been looking into who else had gone into Town Hall and had access to the money.

"Now, what's not obtained legally," Uncle Stanley added, "is the list of employee ID badges that were scanned and the door locations where they were scanned. I have a buddy working on getting us those records."

Marshall covered his ears. "I didn't hear that."

"I doubt the list would be that long anyway," Nina said. "That sort of technology was pretty new back then—or at least new by Tenacity standards. When I was talking to Bridget at one of the football practices, she said they used to prop open some of the doors because the mayor was always forgetting his ID badge."

"Probably was so full of himself, he didn't think he needed to identify himself to anyone, let alone a door," Barrett mumbled as he scrolled on the computer, staring intently at the business license list.

"Still, it wouldn't hurt to see if we can narrow down who was going in and out of the place." Uncle Stanley was right, even if it was a long shot.

Barrett looked up from the screen. "I can't believe Pappy's shut down. And Strike Zone, too? Wasn't that the only bowling alley in the entire county?"

"They tried to expand by incorporating indoor batting cages when they thought more people would be moving here. But the sports-complex concept was still relatively new, and with a loss of tourism, they just couldn't keep things afloat."

"Man, if I had known how bad things had gotten, I would've…" Barrett ran his hand through his hair. "I don't know what I would've done. Or what I could have done. But it's hard not to feel responsible that everything went to pieces when me and my parents disappeared."

"Speaking of your parents, Barrett," Marshall started, then glanced at Stanley, who nodded for him to continue. "Is there any chance that one of them took the money and then hid it, planning to come back for it later?"

Nina would be lying if she said the thought hadn't crossed her mind at least once. But Barrett was shaking his head emphatically.

"No way. If you guys met them, you would see how ludicrous that theory is. My mom is hardly a criminal mastermind. She's so flighty and fidgety, she needs to set a reminder on her phone to switch the clothes from the washer to the dryer. And my dad, well, he probably suffered more than anyone else following our hasty exit from Tenacity." Barrett paused for a few seconds, then shook his head again. "You should have seen him the night we left. This man that I had idolized my entire life as the manliest of men, this man who has been kicked by horses and burned by melted iron and doesn't even flinch from the pain? He openly cried as we drove away, saying he was leaving everything he loved behind. I didn't know my dad had tear ducts because I'd never seen him cry. That killed me to know that my parents' lives were ruined because of me. So, no, leaving Tenacity was the last thing they wanted.

There's no way they would have upended their world like that for no reason."

"Well, if they're interested, it could be beneficial for me to meet with them. I'd really like to get your father's input on how the mayor seemed the evening he came to your house before you all left."

"I can ask him," Barrett said. "But my folks have never been all that comfortable talking about it."

Nina placed her hand gently on Barrett's back. "Maybe they just aren't comfortable talking about it with you?"

"Why wouldn't they be?"

"Sometimes parents think they're protecting their kids by not bringing up a subject they think might trigger bad memories," Marshall suggested.

"Are you a parent?" Barrett asked his attorney.

"I'm not."

"How about this." Stanley folded his hands together. "They don't have to come to Tenacity. I have their address over in Whitehorn. Why don't I stop by and introduce myself? Maybe they'll feel more at ease talking about it in the comfort of their own home with someone who doesn't have any skin in the game, so to speak."

"That might work." Barrett nodded. "Just make sure they know that nobody thinks they're guilty of anything but trying to protect their son."

Obviously, nobody was planning to accuse the Deroys of something more than that. But what was the point of launching a full-blown investigation if they didn't rule out everyone as a potential suspect? Even Nina's own parents weren't exempt. She could tell by the look Marshall and Stanley exchanged that they were in agreement about not ruling anyone out.

When Barrett glanced at the two men, though, Marshall cleared his throat.

"I spoke with the county sheriff's office," Marshall said. "I'm not saying you're in the clear on this yet, Barrett. That's going to be up to the district attorney. But it's starting to look that way."

"Maybe so," Barrett replied. "But I won't feel free until I know who actually committed the crime and why I was framed for it."

Nina couldn't blame him. She for one had put way too much time and energy into solving this case to not actually solve the case.

Barrett wasn't convinced that trying to find out who stole the money wasn't a complete waste of their time. If the local authorities weren't interested, then why was he?

As he and Nina left Marshall's office, they passed the bank where an older woman was walking away from the ATM. Barrett saw Mrs. Ferguson before Nina did and stopped so that she could pass in front of them. Instead of thanking him, though, Mrs. Ferguson clutched her purse to her chest and gave Barrett the side eye as she scooted past him and hurried across the sidewalk.

"Are you serious, Mrs. Ferguson?" Nina put her hands on her hips. "Nobody is going to rob you out here in full daylight."

The woman didn't seem convinced, though, as she kept her eyes trained on him and her infamous middle finger clear of her purse straps in case she felt the need to flash it.

Barrett rubbed the back of his neck, unsure of what else these people wanted from him. He forced a polite smile and tried some lighthearted humor. "Nina's right, ma'am. I prefer to wait until nighttime before robbing people."

Mrs. Ferguson gasped, then shook her head. "You shouldn't be making jokes about theft, Barrett Deroy. People's lives were ruined when that money went missing, and businesses went under. My grandson lost his job and had to move to Helena. Now I hardly ever get to see my great-grandkids."

"That's not Barrett's fault, Mrs. Ferguson," Nina tried to defend him, but Barrett knew it was pointless. Especially because the older woman was already getting into her car after saying her piece.

"At least she didn't flip you off this time," Nina said, frowning at the departing sedan. "I suppose that's progress."

"This town needs a scapegoat." Barrett took her elbow and continued down the sidewalk. "And I'm the easiest one to blame. I'm the outsider."

This time it was Nina who gasped. "You're not an outsider. You grew up in this town, the same as me. You have just as much right to be here as anyone else."

"Except it's not the same town anymore, is it?"

"Again, Barrett, that's not your fault. If anything, Mayor Woodson and the city council should have done a better job of managing things."

"You heard Mrs. Ferguson. Lives were ruined. People moved away. At the end of the day, does it even matter whose fault it was? My being here is a reminder of what people lost. Proving who stole that money might make me feel better, but it's not going to bring back Mrs. Ferguson's grandson. I can run a few football practices, but it's not going to make the town whole again. It's starting to feel like it's too late to fix things in Tenacity. Like it's a lost cause."

"What about us, Barrett?" Nina turned to face him. "Is it too late for the two of us?"

His heart turned heavy, and he couldn't answer. He didn't want to say the wrong thing. Yet he had no idea what the right thing was anymore.

"I know that we haven't been back in each other's lives that long and you've been very careful about not making promises." Nina's eyes looked damp, but her spine was straight and she kept her head held high. "I understand your situation, and that's why I'm not holding you to anything. But at the same time, I don't want to waste my time or hold out hope for something that isn't there. So. Is it too late?"

Barrett ran his hand through his hair. "Nina, you're asking questions that I don't have the answers for."

"No, I'm not. I'm asking you what you're feeling. Right now. Right this second. Do you feel good about us, Barrett? Do you feel like this is something that can work?"

"I want it to work. God, you have no idea how much I want things to work, how much I want things to go back to the way they used to be. But we can't go back."

"Except the whole point of you being here is to go back and revisit the past. In fact, I've been so consumed by this investigation, sometimes it feels as though I'm still living in the past."

"Then you can't ask me to rush through the present and jump right into predicting the future."

"I'm not asking you to predict anything. I'm simply asking where your head is at. Because a few seconds ago, you used the phrase *lost cause*. And before I go back to your room with you, I need to know that you don't think this—" she gestured toward him and then toward herself "—is a lost cause."

"Of course I don't think that. Hell, Nina, spending time with you is the only thing that's made Tenacity bearable. Don't ever doubt for a second how much I care about you."

She slipped her arm into his. "Good. Then we're still on the same page."

Except they weren't.

While they both might've still had intense feelings for each other, Barrett knew that his presence in her life could end up costing her. In fact, he cared about her so much, he wasn't willing to subject her to a life of scrutiny. Because no matter how many times Nina told him she didn't need his protection, he'd spent most of his life trying to shield her in one way or another. Protecting her was the only reason he'd stayed away for so long. He couldn't stop now.

That was why he couldn't answer her about the possibility of a future together. Nothing was certain. Having left his whole world behind him once before, Barrett was only too aware that he wasn't guaranteed a tomorrow with Nina.

Which was why when they returned to the inn, Barrett made love to her with a passion and intensity like it might be their last time together.

Chapter Thirteen

Something had shifted last night.

Nina wasn't sure what it was. But when she woke up this morning in Barrett's arms, she couldn't help but feel like she was past the point of no return.

Last night, she hadn't meant to press him on the issue of their future together. While Nina had been entrenched in this investigation for the past fifteen years, spending so much of her free time going through so many possible scenarios of who'd done it, she needed to remind herself that this wasn't Barrett's normal. He'd had to go into hiding, unable to afford getting caught up in solving the case because he was too busy trying to erase any trace of his past.

He was still wrestling with so much new information when they'd run into Mrs. Ferguson outside of the bank. Yet when the opening came up with his line about things being a lost cause, Nina hadn't been able to stop herself from asking about their future.

Now she regretted that she'd pushed him too soon. It wasn't that he seemed more distant—in fact he'd made love to her like he never wanted to let her go. So then why was she feeling as though she had to give him space?

"I need to leave for work," she said as she eased out of his sleepy embrace. "Do you have plans for today?"

"Actually, I wanted to follow up on Stanley's list of business owners during the time the money went missing." He yawned as she stood to find her discarded clothes, but she could feel his eyes on her. "Then football practice after that."

"That reminds me." Nina made the mistake of turning around before she was fully dressed. Barrett was now sitting up, his chest bare and the lower half of his body covered by only a sheet. It was all she could do not to toss her jeans onto the floor and climb back into bed with him. "I think I've gotten as much info as I can from the football parents. I'm going to hit the Tenacity Quilting Club tonight instead and see if anyone there has some new gossip. Or old gossip. Or any gossip, really."

Barrett's lazy smile was making it hard for her to concentrate. "Since when have you taken up quilting, Nina Sanchez?"

"I can sew," she insisted.

"I know your mom tried to teach you to sew. But you used to hate it."

"No, I just hated how much I sucked at it. I could never get my seams to line up right."

His laughter was warm and husky and way too playful. "That must be so hard for you to come to terms with not being perfect at something."

"Are you calling me a perfectionist, Barrett Deroy?"

"Well, there is certainly one thing you've perfected."

"What's that?"

He lowered the sheet in invitation. "Come back to bed, and I'll show you."

Nina was an hour late to work, but thankfully, she could make up for it by staying later to work with Gladiator, who did well with the steers but would run in the opposite direction every time a heifer came too close to him. She'd barely had time to stop off at home and shower before heading to the Tenacity Quilting Club. It wasn't until she was walking down the basement steps in the Goodness & Mercy Nondenominational Church that she realized she didn't have a project to work on.

She whispered as much to her mom when Nicole Sanchez recovered from the surprise of seeing her not-so-crafty daughter show up unannounced. Her mom pointed to a storage cabinet in the back corner of the room. "Go look in the bins on the bottom shelf. That's where we store the half-done projects that people have given up on."

Nina walked over to the cabinet, relieved that nobody paid much mind to her arriving empty-handed since they were all busy. The club wasn't a traditional sewing circle with everyone working on the same quilt. Each member usually worked on their own things while they socialized and shared advice about anything from quilt templates to bread-pudding recipes to the current topic of conversation, which was the best place to go to get a free tire rotation.

"Once they get your car up in the air," Cecil Brewster argued, "they find all sorts of things that ain't even broke, and it'll end up costing you an arm and a leg. And they don't even offer free doughnuts like the place over in Bronco."

"Is that the place next door to the new nail salon?" Mrs. Castillo asked.

"How should I know, Yolanda?" Cecil lifted his scuffed boots that were probably bought during the last century. "Do I look like the type of man who gets regular pedicures?"

"My Lionel gets pedicures," Norma Parker said. "Lots of men do nowadays."

"I might send Christopher with Lionel next time he goes," Olive Trent offered.

"Well, if Chris and Lionel are going to make a trip out of it," Cecil said with dramatic sigh, "I might as well go along and see what all the fuss is about. Maybe they'd be willing to give us a discount on account of there being three of us cowboys."

Needing to get the image of old man feet from her mind, Nina pulled out several small bins, dismissing each unfinished project as something that was beyond her skill level. When she opened up the last bin shoved way in the back, a wave of nostalgia hit her.

It held a pair of knitting needles, a skein of soft blue yarn, and two-thirds of a scarf she'd started making for Barrett fifteen years ago. When he'd left, she tried to complete it, but each row grew more crooked by the week. Eventually, she'd given up and turned to honing a more useful craft—solving a mystery. She picked up the edges, counting the loops and replaying the steps and motions for a basic garter stitch. Would it feel too symbolic to finally complete the project now? Would Barrett still be in Tenacity when it became cold enough to need a scarf?

It wasn't like Nina had any other options for something to work on. She couldn't just sit around the circle with no purpose but listening to gossip.

By the time she took her bin to an open seat, Nina heard a familiar name that immediately had her ears tingling with promise.

"Cheeto?" her mom asked. "Wasn't that the man who drove the ice-cream truck around the park?"

"Yes," Mrs. Trent said. "I ran into him a couple of weeks ago stocking up at the big-box store in Kalispell. He's got a bigger truck now but still selling ice cream and a whole bunch of other snacks by the looks of his shopping cart."

"I think my kids alone probably racked up a decent

amount of debt with him. Remember, Nina? He used to give you all chips on credit."

"Oh, Nina, I didn't see you slip in," Mrs. Wheaton said, shoving her smudged glasses higher on her nose. "How's our favorite detective doing?"

"I'm doing well, Mrs. Wheaton." Nina smiled, hoping nobody realized that was exactly what she was doing at the quilting club. Detective work.

"I'll say you're doing well," Mrs. Castillo added. "You have that rosy glow about you ever since a certain someone is back in town."

Nina blushed, several women giggled, and Cecil cleared his throat. "Speaking of Tenacity's most famous fugitive, have any of you seen the football practice he's got the boys doing out at the park? We might actually have another shot at State this year if Barrett keeps at it and doesn't skip town again."

"My nephew Grayson is on the team," Carol said. "He can't say enough good things about Barrett Deroy."

Several side conversations broke out about football and Barrett being back in town, but then the elderly Mrs. Wheaton lost her needle and wasn't able to see it on the carpet beneath her chair. Nina tried to help with the search, but her mom ended up having to bring the near-sighted woman another one.

"So, Nina, are the rumors true that you and Barrett are going steady again?" Iris Strom asked.

"I don't know if I'd call it going steady," Nina said.

"I don't think anyone calls it going steady anymore," Carol replied. "I think the kids these days call it hooking up."

"I thought hooking up meant something different," Angela Corey said. "Like it's just a casual sort of thing. With no commitment."

"My grandson says there are apps on the phone now for

people who only want to casually hook up," Mrs. Wheaton offered.

"Nobody's hooking up," Nina's mom said quickly. "Nina
and Barrett are just dating."

"Back in my day," Cecil said, "we called it keeping time
together. Or stepping out together."

"I thought stepping out together meant someone was
cheating," Mrs. Parker said.

"Remember that time Mayor Woodson's wife was stepping out on him?" Mrs. Wheaton asked, and Nina's neck
had never rotated so quickly in her life.

The entire circle went silent, but the woman next to Mrs.
Wheaton made a shushing sound. "Come now, Mildred.
I'm sure June Woodson wasn't stepping out on the mayor."

"Former mayor," Cecil corrected, as though anyone
cared about a small detail like that at a time like this. "And
there's no proof that June actually had an affair with that
ice-cream truck driver."

Wait a second. June Woodson had been having an affair with Cheeto? Or were the older members of the group
getting two separate topics of gossip mixed up?

"No, the affair wasn't with him," Mrs. Wheaton said. "It
was with another guy. A good-looking one. The ice-cream
man just happened to crash into June's car that night they
were caught together."

If Nina had been actively knitting, she would've dropped
her needles. That was how frozen her fingers had grown.
The chill was making its way through the rest of her body,
and she took a steadying breath so that she wouldn't sound
desperate for information. When she felt calm enough, she
said, "I don't remember ever hearing about Cheeto crashing into Brent's mom's car."

Several voices around her voiced the same doubt, making it more likely that this strain of gossip was completely unfounded and unreliable.

"Of course most of you didn't hear about it." Cecil's gnarled fingers remained steady on his quilting square as he spoke confidently. "Woodson got rid of the ice-cream driver so he wouldn't talk."

Carol gasped. "Like, he killed him?"

"He couldn't have killed him," Mrs. Trent said. "Remember I just said I saw him the other day stocking up his new truck."

"The truck that Woodson bought to keep him quiet. Why do you think the man left town so quick with no notice?" Cecil appeared to be oblivious to the shocked faces around him as he continued his stitching.

But then again, so was Mrs. Wheaton, who likely couldn't see anyone's face as she said, "I never liked him as our mayor myself. So controlling of that wife of his and jealous of any man that looked in her direction. I almost don't blame June Woodson for wanting to leave him."

Nina's eyes flew straight to her mother, as though asking for confirmation. But Nicole Sanchez's face showed the same confused expression of most of the people in the room. She then looked to Lucy Bernard, the only other person there who was her age, but Lucy was exchanging stunned glances with her own mother, Elaina.

Nina opened her mouth, but before she could get her question out, the door opened and Victoria Woodson, Brent's younger sister, walked in. "Sorry I'm late. I drove over to the fabric store in Bronco to get more material. Why is everyone so quiet? What did I miss?"

"We were just—" Cecil started.

"Talking about pedicures and the new football team and

Nina's love life." Her mother thankfully interrupted the old man before he could tell Victoria the truth.

Of course, it also put Nina right back in the hot seat. *Thanks a lot, Mom.*

"Nina's love life sounds much more interesting than mine," Victoria said, pulling up a chair next to Nina. "Does this have anything to do with Barrett Deroy coming back to town all sexy and grown up?"

If ever there was a time for her phone to ring or a fire alarm to sound or a stampede of cattle to come tearing across Central Avenue, now was the time.

Nina gulped, forcing a smile on her face, and grasped for any possible answer. "I'm not sure if I'd define it as a love life. We're just seeing each other."

Thankfully, several of the other quick-thinking quilting club members immediately reignited the discussion about different terms used to define the stages of a relationship. This time, though, nobody uttered the words *stepping out.*

"Is that a scarf?" Victoria asked, politely smiling at the tangles of yarn in Nina's lap.

"It was. But I got the pattern twisted a few times, and now it seems like I'm just making a mess out of it."

"It happens to the best of us," Victoria said with a knowing smile.

Somehow it felt like neither one of them was talking about scarves or knitting. Or maybe that was just Nina's overactive imagination. After all, she'd just been bombarded with more possible leads than she could process. This investigation was getting more and more complicated, and it was becoming increasingly difficult to keep all the loops and knots in order.

Focus, she told herself. But the thing that kept popping into her mind was that Barrett wasn't the first person Cliff

Woodson had run out of town. Or at least strongly advised to leave. What exactly had Cheeto seen that night he'd crashed into June Woodson's car? Had Barrett also witnessed something he wasn't supposed to see, and that was why the former mayor accused him of stealing the money? Was it truly part of some elaborate setup?

Wow. This was huge.

"Excuse me." Nina stood up, leaving the yarn and needles on the chair she'd just vacated. "I need to get a snack."

"A word of warning since you're new to Quilting Club." Victoria used a finger to motion Nina closer. When she leaned in, Nina's heart thudded as she waited for the younger Woodson to issue some sort of threat to stop investigating her family. Instead she whispered, "Stay away from the caramel-popcorn balls until after you finish your project. Mrs. Wheaton uses way too much corn syrup, and your fingers will end up sticking to that yarn. One time, Cecil's fabric was practically glued to his right hand and it took three ladies, two pairs of scissors, and a gallon of dish soap to get it off him."

Nina could only manage a polite chuckle in response. She made her way to the table laid out with treats that the members brought from home to share, noting that the popcorn balls hadn't been touched. She was hungry, because she always seemed to be hungry, but her real reason for excusing herself was because she needed to text Barrett. She couldn't wait to ask him what he knew about the Woodsons' alleged marital problems.

When she pulled out her phone, she saw a message from him.

I'm going to ride with Marshall to Rust Creek Falls tonight. We have a meeting first thing tomorrow with one of the former city clerks. Your uncle found out that she moved

from Tenacity soon after my family left. Get this, she's
currently on probation for embezzlement from a different government office. Wish us luck.

Wow. That was a pretty big lead. And if it turned out
that the former clerk had a history of embezzlement, then
all this new speculation about Mayor Woodson trying to
cover up an affair could be chalked up to unsubstantiated
gossip and quickly forgotten.

Nina inhaled deeply through her nose. In fact, she
wanted to forget the possible scandal already. Being privy
to the sensationalized details of a true crime case involving complete strangers was one thing. But the allegations
she'd heard tonight were about people she knew, people
their community looked up to and respected.

Nina suddenly felt the need to take a shower and…what?
Wash out her ears? Erase all trace of ever hearing such a
scandalous thing about the former first family of Tenacity?

The problem was that she couldn't forget what had just
been said.

As much as she hoped that Barrett and Marshall's new
lead would solve the mystery, Nina also knew that she
couldn't overlook this. No matter how much she didn't
want to believe it. She glanced over her shoulder and saw
Victoria chatting to Carol and Mrs. Strom.

It wasn't like she could sit back down and ask Victoria
if *she* knew anything about her mom having an affair and
her dad paying off people to leave town. Maybe it wasn't
just Barrett and Cheeto the mayor had run off.

Maybe it was also the man his wife had been cheating
on him with…

A wave of dizziness spiraled through Nina, and she had
to put a hand on the snack table to steady herself.

A hazy memory suddenly flashed through her mind—a memory she must have blocked out. Or it could be that she was just so desperate to solve this case, she was starting to imagine things. Nina needed to get out of this room with all the voices and the gossip and Victoria's eyes now looking in this direction.

She still had her phone in her hand, so she quickly held it up to her ear and pretended like she was taking a call. Grabbing her purse, Nina mumbled something to her mother on her way out the door. By the time she got to her car and shut herself inside, her pulse was pounding and she was sucking in gulps of air.

She took several deep breaths and closed her eyes, trying to concentrate on the memory she'd suppressed before now.

It had been a couple of months before her fourteenth birthday, and Nina had just found out that her parents were planning a road trip that summer to drive to Mexico to visit extended family. She'd asked them if Barrett could go with them, and they hadn't said yes but they also hadn't said no—which was pretty much the same thing as saying yes in Nina's young mind. She had snuck out of her house to go tell Barrett that he might be invited. As she rounded the corner to his property, though, she heard voices coming from inside the small outbuilding that Mr. Deroy used as a workshop. She recognized Barrett's dad's voice, and because it wasn't unusual for him to be working in his shop late at night, she didn't pay any attention to what he was saying. However, the other voice was more hushed, more desperate, and most definitely not Barrett's mom.

I'm going to leave him, Bear! He's jealous and controlling, and I can't stand it one more day...

Nina had no idea who the voice belonged to—she only knew that it wasn't a conversation she was meant to hear.

She'd also seen that there wasn't a light on in Barrett's window, so she'd turned around and run straight home.

Now she wondered if the woman she'd heard had been…

No. She wasn't going to jump to any conclusions. Surely, someone else would know who Barrett's dad might have been talking to that night. Or know who would've called the man by such an intimate nickname.

And what was that Luca had said the other night at Sunday dinner? Something about the Deroys always conveniently going out of town.

At first, Nina had taken it as a dig on Barrett's entire family leaving town. But now she was remembering how often Barrett Senior had to travel for work. Not that it meant he was having an affair, she quickly reminded herself as she scrolled through her contacts list and found Luca's name.

She quickly texted her brother to find out if he was available. He responded and said he was at the Grizzly. Good. Nina started the engine. Maybe she could also talk to Dale while she was there. See if he remembered anything.

Chapter Fourteen

Unfortunately, when Nina walked into the Grizzly Bar, she saw that her brother was sitting with Brent Woodson and Noah Trent watching a baseball game on the TV over the bar.

"Uh-oh." Brent smiled as she walked toward the table. "Does your boyfriend know you're consorting with the enemy?"

"Are you and Barrett still beefing?" Noah, whose family owned Stargazer Ranch, asked Brent before Nina could answer. "They found the missing money already. I thought you two were moving on from all that and working together to coach the football team."

"It's complicated," Brent said.

"It's not that complicated," Luca told Noah, then took a swig of his beer. "They're both stuck in the past and acting like they're still competing for homecoming king."

Noah lifted a brow at her as though asking her to confirm Luca's analysis. Nina sighed. "It's not quite as simple as that, but yeah. It would be nice if they could work together to put the past behind them."

Nina had initially hoped Brent would eventually come around to helping Barrett clear his name as a sort of atonement for not sticking up for him in high school. But if Nina's suspicions about their parents were correct, then there was going to be a much bigger obstacle in the way of them ever becoming friends.

"I'm not the one still holding a grudge, Nina," Brent said.

"Really?" Nina put her hands on her hips. "The grudge seemed to be on full display at the Fourth of July fireworks."

"I'd had a bit too much to drink." Brent held up a glass that looked like it contained iced tea. "I've been cutting back."

"What about the next night when Luca showed up at the Social Club to tell Barrett you and some friends were looking for him? Was the grudge still active after you sobered up?"

"For me? Not as much. I quickly came to the realization that it took a lot of guts for Deroy to come back to town the way he did. I doubt a guilty man would've showed up like that. For my dad, though? The grudge is still there. He was the one who asked me to speak to Barrett and find out what he was doing in town. I figured the questions would sound better coming from me than from the sheriff."

"Why would your dad still be holding a grudge against a teenage boy?" Nina asked.

"Nina." Luca's low voice was issuing a warning.

"You'd have to ask my dad." Brent shoved away from the table and stood up. "Now, if you'll excuse me, the pool table just opened up and I've got next game."

As he walked away, she opened her mouth to call out another question, but her brother's voice was even more insistent. "I said drop it, Nina."

"I'm going to call Lucy and check on the triplets." Noah stood up as though he couldn't get away from the table quick enough.

Nina collapsed into the seat Noah had just vacated. "Why do you always do that, Luca?"

"Do what?" Her brother finished the beer in his mug. "Save you from making a fool out of yourself?"

"No. Save yourself from ever having to actually take a side."

"Because maybe there might be more sides to this situation than you think."

She scooted her chair closer and lowered her voice. "You know something that you're not telling me."

Luca rolled his eyes. "Jeez, Nina. If you wanted to be a detective, you should've gone to the police academy. At least then you'd be able to solve real crimes."

"See. Why would you say this isn't a real crime unless you know something?"

"Look, I get it that you want closure for your boyfriend. But sometimes when you ask too many questions, you get answers you aren't ready to face."

His words were cryptic enough to confirm that he was probably aware of the alleged scandal she'd just heard about tonight. The open-ended questions weren't working, which meant she had to cut to the chase and go with her hunch. "Did you know that June Woodson and Barrett Deroy Senior were having an affair?"

"Shhhh!" Luca's face darkened as he scanned the room. "This isn't a good place to talk about that, Nina."

"Well, the Tenacity Quilting Club probably wasn't a good place for Cecil Brewster to bring it up either. But clearly he isn't as concerned about the Woodsons' reputations as you are."

"I'm concerned about my best friend finding out the truth about his dad."

"So what is the truth, Luca? Did his and June's relationship have something to do with why the Deroys left town?"

"The truth is that I'm not talking about this with you

anymore, Nina. I was sixteen when things went down. I didn't want to think about it then and I don't want to think about it now. The money has been found. Barrett is no longer a suspect." Luca wiped imaginary dust off his hands. "All's well that ends well."

With that, her brother left to join Brent and Noah at the pool table. Nina knew by her brother's reaction that the thing she didn't want to think was possible was becoming more probable. Brent's mom and Barrett's dad had an affair, and the mayor found out about it. What better way to get your wife's lover out of the way than to stage a crime? Maybe Barrett wasn't supposed to be the fall guy—his dad was.

Nina rubbed the throbbing spot at her temple. If all of this was true, how was she going to tell Barrett?

Barrett had only been gone from Tenacity for twenty-four hours, but he was already missing Nina more than he'd thought possible. Especially considering he had once missed her a lot longer than twenty-four hours before.

The drive back with Marshall was quiet. The former city employee they'd talked to had a solid alibi for when the money had gone missing—she'd been in Hawaii blowing through some other embezzled funds she'd made from her time as a youth leader in charge of cookie sales.

I only worked in Tenacity for a few months, the former employee had told Barrett and Marshall over breakfast at the Gold Rush Diner. *That wife of the mayor's kept that cashier's office locked up tighter than a steel drum. What she should have done was put all that cash in the bank. But it was clear that whoever was supposed to be in charge of that money wasn't doing things by the book. I knew right away that someone else had designs on the restoration fund and I wasn't going to be able to touch a penny of it.*

So I helped myself to the cookie sales instead and hopped a plane to Maui.

When the woman left, Barrett paid for breakfast, and then he and Marshall both double-checked their wallets to make sure their cash and bank cards were still in place.

"It would've made things nice and easy to find out that she was the culprit," Barrett said when they stopped for gas.

"Yep." Marshall nodded. "But if it was that easy, then someone would've pointed the finger at her before now."

That was a fair point. In fact, with so much time having passed and so little interest left for this case, maybe Barrett would never be able to figure out who stole the money. He said as much to Marshall when the man returned from the convenience store with two sodas and a bag full of road-trip snacks that would make a minivan full of ten-year-olds envious.

Marshall passed a pack of gum to Barrett. "The truth will come out when it comes out, I guess."

"Now you're sounding like Winona," Barrett told his attorney. "I guess I should just be glad that I'm officially off the hook."

Marshall had received a call from the district attorney's office right before breakfast. They confirmed that they had no intention of filing charges against Barrett—or anyone else—since the money was recovered and there was no proof of any crime.

"You know what I thought was odd, though?" Marshall asked when they pulled back onto the highway. "What she said about June Woodson keeping the cashier's office locked up so tight. And how it was obvious to her, a career criminal, that someone else was already laying the groundwork for the same heist."

"The past two weeks, my head has been spinning with scenarios and possibilities." Barrett made an explosion sound. "To be honest with you, man, this investigation business is not for me. I just want to take care of my horses and split a cast-iron-skillet meal with Nina."

Marshall offered him half of a Twix bar. "And run some football drills?"

Barrett looked at the clock on his dashboard. "Right. We better hurry if I'm going to make it to practice on time."

Three hours and two sugar highs later, Barrett was setting up cones in the park when he saw Nina striding across the grass toward him.

Actually, she wasn't striding so much as walking painfully steady as though she had to force herself to put one foot in front of the other. Barrett knew that she hadn't been happy the other night when he'd told her that he wasn't ready to fully invest in a relationship until he cleared his name. Boy, he'd sounded like such a jerk assuming that she would want to wait around for him as though they hadn't already waited fifteen years to finally be together.

Hopefully, what he was about to tell her would put a smile back on her face. As soon as she was within arm's reach, Barrett picked her up and whirled her around.

She shrieked, but the smile returned to her face and Barrett was never going to do anything to make her doubt how he felt about her again. When he finally set her down, she said, "Thank goodness the trip to Rust Creek Falls was a success. Did she come right out and admit to stealing the money?"

"No." Barrett was grinning like a fool.

"Did she point the finger at who did?"

"No."

Nina's smile slipped. "Then the trip *wasn't* a success?"

"No, it was," Barrett said. "Just not in that way."

"In what way, then?"

He'd forgotten that Nina had spent much of her adult life

trying to solve this mystery. She'd been so focused on all the small details, it was probably hard for her to see things from a bigger picture. Which meant that she wasn't going to expect him to say the following words to her. "The DA all but exonerated me. There won't be any charges."

Her smile returned and she blinked several times before throwing herself back into his arms. "Finally! This is the best news I've had…well, since you came back to Tenacity. No, it's better than that day."

"I know." He kissed her, then set her down so that he could hold her head in his hands and look at her face. "We should get married."

Nina's mouth flew open, and he almost laughed at her shocked expression.

"Sorry—I meant that to come out a little more romantically. I know we're still getting used to each other again, and I'm not trying to put a timetable on anything. But the whole drive back I've been dying to tell you that I missed you and want to be with you."

"What happened to wanting to clear your name first?" Nina's brows drew together as she studied his face.

Barrett shrugged. "It finally dawned on me that we may never be able to figure out what happened. I know you've put so much time and energy and years of work into investigating this case, and I appreciate that. Lord, Nina, you will never know how much I appreciate that. Your commitment and determination have made me realize that it doesn't matter what other people think about me. If you're in my corner, I don't need anything else. I'm tired of putting my life on hold. I want you. Do you want me?"

Nina nodded, her eyes filled with unshed tears. Her smile was wide, but it was also stiff, as if she was trying to hold something back.

"What is it?" He wiped a teardrop from her cheek.

"I'm so happy," she said. "The past fifteen years, I haven't allowed myself to dream for a moment just like this. I have never stopped wanting you, Barrett."

"But?"

"I'm getting everything I wanted...everything except proving your innocence."

Just a few moments earlier, he'd been praising her determination and commitment. Now he was wondering if he could simultaneously be frustrated by it.

"If *I'm* fine with not proving my innocence, then you should be fine with it, too. I thought you would be happy that I no longer want to put things on hold."

"A couple of days ago, that would have been the case." She was still hesitating. This wasn't the Nina he knew.

"So tell me what changed."

She bit her lower lip. "I was really hoping that whoever you and Marshall were meeting would be the one who stole the money. Because I didn't want to have to tell you what I'm about to tell you." Her words hit him with a force.

"You found out something and weren't going to tell me?"

"Of course I was going to tell you. Eventually. I was just going to..." She sucked in her cheeks and then exhaled deeply. "I was just going to try to confirm a few things first. But it's been lies that have kept us apart all this time, and I'm not convinced that anyone else is going to come out and admit what I think really happened. I should also add that most of what I'm about to tell you is allegations and speculations—except when I put it all together with my own memories, it does add up. Unfortunately."

"Nina." He was trying hard to be patient, but once again he felt like a naive sixteen-year-old being kept in the dark. "Just tell me."

"Last night I was at the Tenacity Quilting Club, and some-one brought up Cheeto and the real reason he left town."

"The ice-cream-truck man?"

"Yes. *Allegedly*—" she emphasized the word, and he had to wonder if she had her own doubts about whatever story she'd pieced together "—Cheeto crashed his truck into a car one night. Inside the car was June Woodson and a per-son she was possibly having an affair with."

"Oh wow." Barrett's eyes widened. Now she had his at-tention. "The mayor's wife? She was *possibly* having an affair, or she *was* having an affair?"

"Yes, the mayor's wife. And I can't tell you what exactly they were doing in the car because I wasn't there."

"Right. You did say *allegedly*. So Cheeto wasn't the one having the affair with the mayor's wife?"

"No." Nina scrunched her nose. "He was just driving the vehicle that crashed into the couple."

"But for some reason, Cheeto left town after catching the mayor's wife having an affair." Barrett ran his hand through his hair. "I'm guessing that this means my family weren't the only ones the mayor has pushed out of Tenacity."

"According to my sources, Cliff Woodson paid him off in exchange for not saying anything about the affair."

"Your sources?" Barrett asked.

Nina waved a dismissive hand. "That's not the impor-tant part."

Barrett disagreed, but they could get to that later. "So Cheeto left town, and what happened to June and her mys-tery lover? I'm assuming things didn't work out between them since she and the mayor are still together."

"That's the same thing I concluded. Things didn't work out between them because Mr. Woodson also ran the other man out of town."

"Ha." Barrett made the sound despite not finding the slightest bit of humor in the situation. "Sounds like the guy probably deserved it, sleeping with another man's wife. How did the mayor manage to get rid of the poor chump?"

Nina's gaze was so steady as it held his, he didn't see her slip her hand into his palm until he felt her fingers squeezing his. "The mayor accused the other man's teenage son of stealing the town's renovation fund."

It took several heartbeats before Barrett felt the pounding in his ears. Nina couldn't possibly be saying… She nodded, as though she could hear the doubt screaming inside his brain.

"You think *my* dad was having an affair with June Woodson?"

"Yes."

"*My* dad?"

"I know that this is hard for you to believe, Barrett, but surely you can see how something like this could happen."

"I can't see how anything like this could happen," he replied a bit too defensively. "My father might've been a ladies' man at one time, but we're talking about June Woodson, here. The mother and politician's wife who would never so much as belch in public let alone engage in a scandalous love affair with a married man."

"My sources said—"

"Who?" He interrupted her. "Who are your sources?"

"Cecil and Mrs. Wheaton brought it up at the quilting club."

"Your sources are an old busybody cowboy and a woman with bad eyesight?"

"I also overheard your dad talking to a woman once in the workshop behind your house. At the time, I didn't recognize the voice, but I knew it wasn't your mom. She was telling him that her husband was jealous and controlling and she planned to leave him."

"You heard my dad having a midnight tryst in the shop behind my house, under my mom's nose, and you never told me about it before now?"

"I didn't remember it until I was at the quilting club and people started talking about an affair. Look, Barrett, I know you're finding this hard to believe, but don't you see that this is the former mayor's motive for taking the money and making it look like you stole it?"

"It could be the motive, Nina. Or it could be that you're grasping at straws to clear my name."

She took a step back as though he'd struck her.

"I don't mean that in a bad way," he tried to clarify. "All I'm saying is that you don't always have to fight for something. Not everything is a mystery that needs to be solved."

"Trust me, this is one mystery I wish would have stayed long buried."

"Then why didn't you let it stay buried? You said it was alleged gossip and that you couldn't even confirm it. Why couldn't you have just told me that you were satisfied with me not clearing my name?"

"I tried to," she said, but he barely heard her over the battle of emotions now raging inside of him.

"Or maybe you've never really believed me and will only be convinced if you get more proof. No matter who gets in the way."

Nina winced, and this time he was the one who took a step back, needing some distance so he could think without saying something else he would regret.

But he didn't have the luxury of thought. He had fifteen teenagers about to head his way to practice football drills.

Nina lifted her chin. "If you don't believe me, then you can ask Luca what he remembers."

"Aw hell," her brother said as he walked up behind them. "You told him."

"Did you know about this?" Barrett asked his one-time best friend. But he could see from the pity reflected in Luca's eyes that Nina wasn't the only one who believed that Barrett Deroy Senior was capable of—

No. Barrett wasn't willing to contemplate the worst about his own father without talking to the man himself.

Someone dropped what sounded like eighty pounds of shoulder pads to the left of Barrett and said, "Mrs. Vandergrift may be retired, but she still has the master key to the high school. I was able to sweet-talk her into letting us into the athletic storage unit to get some equipment."

Barrett nearly roared when he saw that the newcomer was Brent Woodson. "You knew about this, too?"

"Did you think it was a secret that you always hold practice at three?" Brent asked. "Or do you mean did I know about Principal Vandergrift's master key?"

Luca shook his head. "He doesn't know, Barrett."

It was bad enough thinking of Brent Woodson as the mayor's heir apparent. The golden son of Tenacity. But looking at his slightly confused face, all Barrett could see was June Woodson's son.

"Know what?" Brent asked.

Right now, the only way to regain an ounce of his dwindling self-respect was by not repeating the gossip.

"That you're taking over practice." Barrett threw the ball to Brent. "I'm out of here."

Chapter Fifteen

Less than an hour ago, Nina thought she and Barrett Deroy were going to be married. Now she wasn't even sure if they'd be speaking by night's end. He stormed away from practice, leaving a trail of confusion in his angry wake before driving off.

Luckily, Brent didn't ask Nina or Luca why his former rival was hell-bent on turning over coaching duties—which was for the best because Nina didn't think she could tell another grown man that his parent had been having an affair.

"I'm sure he'll be back," Luca said as Brent passed out shoulder pads to the arriving members of the team.

"Will he?" Nina sniffed, trying to keep her tears at bay.

"He loves you," Luca said.

The funny thing was that was the one thing Barrett *hadn't* said earlier when he suggested they get married. It wasn't that she necessarily doubted his feelings for her, but she had never seen him this angry.

People changed. Everyone had warned her. She'd even seen the harsh look of resentment in Barrett's eyes the night he returned to town and nearly got into a brawl with Brent Woodson. Unfortunately, this time, his wrath had been directed at Nina.

"I should have listened to you," she told her brother. "I should have dropped it and left well enough alone."

"Damn right you should have," Luca said, then shrugged. "But we both knew there was no way in hell you were going to do that."

"Then tell me what I should do now, my wise big brother. How do I fix the mess I've made?"

"By finishing, little sister." Luca patted the top of her head in the most annoyingly patronizing way. "By closing the case. You have all the facts. Now you need to prove them so you can hold someone accountable. Don't forget— you're not just solving this for Barrett. You're solving it for every person whose life turned sideways when the money went missing. You're solving it for Tenacity."

Twenty minutes later, Nina pulled into the driveway of Winona and Uncle Stanley's rental home they used when they weren't in Bronco.

"What brings you here at this time of night?" her uncle asked.

"I think I may have lost Barrett for good." Nina would've cringed at the defeated tone in her voice, but she didn't even have the emotional energy to do that.

"See, Stan, I told you we were having company tonight." The timer on the oven dinged, and Winona pulled out a cast-iron skillet. "I figured you might need some comfort food when you got here."

Nina looked at her uncle to ask how his wife knew these things, but she might as well ask a bird how they knew to fly south for the winter. They sat at the small kitchen table, and Nina told them what she'd heard at the quilting club and what she'd been able to piece together from her own recently recalled memories. "I made the mistake of telling

Barrett my suspicions, and he accused me of grasping at straws to clear his name."

"People never like the messenger when it's bad news." Winona put another chunk of warm cornbread on Nina's plate without commenting how quickly the piece was devoured. The older woman's bracelets jangled as she passed the crock of honey butter. "It happens to me all the time. They *think* they want answers, but when it's not what they were hoping to hear, they get all bent out of shape."

Uncle Stanley reached over and patted Nina's hand. "Winona is right. Barrett needed to hear the truth. It was better coming from you than it would be coming from someone else in town. Can you imagine if Woodson was the one who told him?"

"No, I can't. In fact, when he stormed off, he practically threw the football right at Brent's head. If the guy hadn't caught it, he would've wound up seeing stars."

"Stars." Winona closed her eyes, and her head tilted to one side, then the other. "It is written in the stars…"

Nina lifted a brow at her uncle, who seemed unfazed by his wife's behavior.

"Stars," she repeated again. Then simply said, "Mayor Woodson."

Her uncle finally spoke up. "No, Winona. Nina said *Brent* Woodson almost saw stars. Not Cliff. You're thinking of the wrong man."

"Wrong man," Winona added to whatever she was trying to say about stars and the mayor. It was hard to understand because the older woman was swaying in her chair and seemed to be repeating herself.

"The note," Nina said suddenly. "Remember the note we found with the money? It said we had the wrong man."

And just like that, Winona straightened and opened her eyes. "Yes. Mayor Woodson was the wrong man."

She then took a bite of her cornbread as though she hadn't just been communicating with some other psychic realm. Nina wasn't sure how any of this worked, but she also knew they wouldn't have gotten this far in the case if it hadn't been for Winona's initial predictions.

"You mean Barrett is the wrong man because he didn't take the money?" Nina asked, hoping for some clarity.

"Of course Barrett is the wrong man," Winona said. "We all knew that already. But the note was telling us that Mayor Woodson was also the wrong man."

"Damn." Uncle Stanley shook his head. "I really had the former mayor pegged for it."

"I don't understand," Nina said. "If it wasn't the mayor who stole the money, then who did? Who else was trying to frame Barrett?"

Barrett hadn't warned his parents that he was coming home to Whitehorn. He'd already made the long drive from Rust Creek Falls to Tenacity today. He was now flying down the highway fueled by adrenaline and the need for confrontation.

He tried to keep his mind focused on every sacrifice his parents had made for him, on every happy childhood memory they'd provided. The problem was that most of his core memories were centered around being with the Sanchez family. And the more good times he remembered, the more he found himself wondering where his own folks had been.

It wasn't that they were absent parents, even though his father had traveled for work quite a bit. It was just that they always seemed focused on their own issues. But Barrett had been too young to ever worry about what those issues might be. Money constraints? Obviously. Job stress? Probably. Relationship problems? Maybe.

He never considered his folks to be as in love as Mr. and Mrs. Sanchez were, but who wanted to think about their own parents in that way at all?

Obviously his dad was capable of love. He'd told Nina, Marshall, and Stanley about the night they'd left town and how his dad had cried saying that he was leaving everything he loved behind.

Except his son and his wife—the two people he should have loved more than anything—were going with him. So what—or who—else had he loved?

June Woodson.

The day Barrett had gone with his dad to town hall to renew the business license was probably the only time Barrett had ever seen his father with the mayor's wife. Except now that he thought more about it, he hadn't really seen them interacting with each other that day either.

He'd seen his dad go into a closed office with a very prim and proper June after saying, *Mrs. Woodson needs me to fill out some forms and what not, son. It might be a while if you want to go down to the pharmacy and grab some ice cream while you wait for me.*

There was the time his dad's truck and work trailer were gone and Barrett had walked in on his mom in his dad's workshop, sitting on the anvil near the cold, empty fire ring. She was holding a scrap of red satin in her hand and staring off into space. When his mom got that look in her eyes, it was best to just get her to bed and leave her with a cool washcloth and a big glass of water next to her prescription bottle. So that was what Barrett had done. But even back then he remembered thinking it was weird for his mom to be holding something made of fabric that had no business being in a blacksmith shop.

Maybe Nina had been right and his father had met June in the workshop for illicit trysts. It would sure explain why his dad had so many questions about the Woodsons when Barrett finally returned to Tenacity.

Barrett stopped for more gas and a large cup of coffee an hour outside of Whitehorn and decided that it was too late to confront anyone tonight. He might as well go straight to his ranch and check on the progress of the water-pipe repairs.

He tossed and turned for several hours before finally falling asleep just before dawn. When he woke up in his own bed, Barrett's first thought was that the last time he'd slept here, Nina had slept beside him. His second thought was that he smelled the distinct aroma of frying bacon, yet he was pretty sure he and Nina had already cooked the package they'd bought at the store.

Barrett pulled on a shirt as he padded out of his bedroom and headed toward the kitchen. Barrett Deroy Senior was standing at the stove holding a pair of tongs. It was almost an unspoken tradition that anytime his dad returned from a work trip, he would always make breakfast. He jokingly called it bringing home the bacon.

This morning, though, Barrett wasn't in the mood for a happy family reunion. "What are you doing here?"

His father exhaled slowly. "When I saw your truck high-tailing it through town late last night, I figured you were hell-bent on something. That was right after I got a phone call from my buddy Cheeto saying an old man named Stanley Sanchez had shown up at his front door. It was the same fella who's been trying to get in touch with me and your mom recently. So I figured you probably had some questions and it might be best if we don't talk in front of your mother."

Barrett's heart sank. He almost didn't even ask, because what more was there for his dad to say? He'd all but confirmed that he was guilty of something. Did it even matter at this point?

Yet if Nina were here, she would want to ask one thing. "Why?"

"Why did I carry on with June Woodson?" his dad asked as he removed the bacon from the pan and put it on a paper towel covered plate to drain. "Because I love her."

Barrett noticed that his father used the present tense. He still loved June. Likely more than he loved his own wife. Possibly more than he loved his own son.

"No. Why did you let people think that I stole money from the city?"

"I had no choice, son. You have to understand what me and Junie were up against."

"Do I, though? You cheated on Mom. This other woman cheated on her husband. What were you two really up against? The solemn vows you both made to other people?" Barrett swallowed the sour taste in his mouth. "Also, can we please not call Mrs. Woodson Junie?"

"She's always been my Junie. Since way before you were born, kid. And she always will be."

"What about Mom?"

"Your mom and I love each other in our own way. She promised me that she would make the best of our situation, but it's been a struggle for us."

"I'll say."

His father turned off the flame on the stove. "Barrett, I came over here to talk to you man to man. If anyone should understand the way things are between me and June, it should be you."

"Okay, Dad, you can save the 'man to man' bravado for when you're in your own house. This is *my* house. It's hard for me to give you credit for finally deciding to come clean about your secret affair after you'd already been tipped off that I knew. But I will say that I'm curious why you think that *I* of all people should be understanding."

Barrett Senior walked to the kitchen table and put his hand, a hand that looked like an older scarred version of Barrett's own, on the back of the chair. "Do you mind if I sit down? Seeing as how this is *your* house and I'm just a guest."

Instead of being sidetracked into an argument over hospitality, Barrett crossed his arms over his chest impatiently.

"You see, I met Junie when her family bought the ranch where my daddy worked."

"In Tenacity?"

"That's right. She might have lived in the big house while I lived in a two-room cabin, but she was my neighbor girl, just like you had a little neighbor girl that you used to be sweet on."

"You're talking about Nina?" So *that* was the connection his father thought they shared? They both had childhood sweethearts. That was why Barrett should be more understanding of such a profound betrayal that ruined so many lives? Although he hadn't been lying when he admitted being curious. He took a seat and nodded at the one across from him.

"Yes." His father sat down. "Junie was to me what Nina was to you."

"Please, Dad. You couldn't possibly know what Nina

means to me. You couldn't even remember her name a few weeks ago."

"When you're as old as me, son, and you've been kicked in the head shoeing horses," his father tapped the side of his scalp, "then you can compare your memory to mine. Now, I'm not saying that our situations were exactly the same. Junie was an only child and didn't have a bunch of protective big brothers. And I had absolutely no sports talent and no hope of ever going to college. I knew that if I had any shot of getting her parents to approve of her marrying someone like me, I had to go out and make a killing on the rodeo circuit."

Barrett knew how that had turned out. His father had always been good with horses but not so much with the bulls, which was where he thought the big money was.

"Now, keep in mind that this was before everyone had cell phones and email to keep in touch. I left Tenacity determined to prove myself." His father's once broad shoulders seemed more stooped. "But I ended up busted up in the hospital more times than I could count and saw my goal slipping away from me."

"And what goal was that?"

"Becoming the man I thought she deserved. But in my foolish, prideful youth, I made the mistake of thinking she'd be sitting around waiting for me to come back to Tenacity to claim her. So when I did finally return, beat down and more broke than I'd been when I left, Junie'd thought I'd given up on us and had already married Cliff. I tried to stay away from her, honest I did. But imagine how you would have felt if you went back to Tenacity to be with your Nina, and you'd found out that she'd already gotten married to someone else. Tell me you wouldn't have been just as heartsick as I had been all those years ago."

The truth was that Barrett *had* imagined exactly that scenario—returning to town only to find out that Nina was gone to him forever. It was a big part of the reason he'd stayed away. If it was true that his father and June had loved each other that much…

Wait.

Barrett wasn't going to let him off that easily. "Dad, I never should have been forced to leave Tenacity *or* Nina in the first place. I didn't choose to leave her the way you chose to leave your girlfriend. Besides, why did you marry Mom if you were still so in love with Mrs. Woodson? Couldn't she have just left her husband for you? It wasn't like divorce was unheard of back then."

"She was already pregnant with Little Brent."

"Okay, I am definitely going to need you to never call him Little Brent again."

"I'm not saying I was the best husband or that Junie and I went about things the right way. But your mom knew where my heart was at when she met me. Dating her was supposed to be a casual thing, something to take my mind off the woman I couldn't be with. It may have been a self-ish attitude for me to have, but I was always honest about it. When I got your mom pregnant, she insisted we get married. I was fine with it because I couldn't have Junie anyway and I had always wanted to be a dad."

Barrett wasn't sure how he was supposed to feel about being an unexpected arrival with his parents making the best of an untimely situation. "Thank you, I guess?"

"But like I said, Junie and I were too in love, and being away from each other only made us want each other more."

Now *that* Barrett could relate to. Seeing Nina after all these years had hit him the same way. Except unlike his father, both he and Nina were still single.

His father continued talking. "The first time Junie and I got caught, I thought that finally we'd both be able to get divorces. But Cliff threatened to sue for full custody of Little Brent, and even though I knew your mom would be more amenable to splitting custody of you, I had just started my farrier business and was traveling around quite a bit. I knew being on the road, going from rodeo to ranch, from ranch to rodeo, was no life for a baby. So Junie and I stayed in our marriages. Until the next time."

"Are we really going to go through the entire sixteen years of your love affair?" Barrett asked. "Or can we skip to the part where her husband stole the town-renovation fund and threatened to blame your son unless you left town for good?"

His father scratched the stubble on his chin. "What makes you think Cliff stole the money?"

"Because he was trying to set you up to take the fall?"

"I wish that had been the case, son. But the truth is that Junie actually stole it. She couldn't take another day being married to that man, and she was planning to use it to hire an attorney and get custody of her daughter. You and Little Brent were old enough by then that if we left town together, you'd both be able to come visit us. But Victoria was still too young."

"Wait. You're telling me that your girlfriend stole the money so that you guys could be together? You knew about it, yet you let your sixteen-year-old son take the blame?"

"I didn't have a choice. Cliff knew she'd been the one to take it. When he confronted her, she had no choice but to admit it. But that wasn't good enough for the power-hungry Mayor Woodson. He'd been humiliated. Having his wife prosecuted for theft would be one more humiliation that would reflect badly on his next campaign. So he did the cruelest thing possible. He figured out a way to punish her by banishing the man she loved."

"Explain to me how blaming *me* for stealing the money would banish *you*, Dad."

"Cliff knew that if he blamed me for it, I'd take the fall for Junie. I might serve a couple of years in prison, but eventually I'd come back to be with her. Instead, he came up with the idea to accuse you. He showed me and your mom the proof he'd already falsified that listed you being in town hall the day it went missing. That was how he tied my hands. He knew that there was no way I would let my son go to jail for a crime he didn't commit. He told me that if we left town, he wouldn't send his prosecutors after you."

So that explained why a formal investigation had never been launched. Mayor Woodson hadn't wanted anyone to find out it was really his own wife who'd taken the money. But why hadn't Barrett's father ever told him that nobody actually had any proof linking him to the crime? Or that there was never really an investigation?

"So you knew your mistress stole the money—"

"Don't call her that, son."

"What would Mom call her?" Barrett shot back.

"I've never kept my love for Junie a secret from your mom. I'm not saying that she gave us her blessing exactly, but I'm not the only one who broke vows during our marriage."

Barrett gritted his teeth, then had to force himself to unclench his jaw. There had been so many revelations in the past sixteen hours, the last thing he wanted to hear was that his mother had been unfaithful as well.

"Look, Dad, I'm trying to accept the fact that you love this other woman and want to protect her. But what about me? You don't want people to think of June Woodson as your mistress, but you've been perfectly fine the past fifteen years letting everyone in Tenacity think your son is a thief."

"I did protect you, Barrett. I gave up Junie to protect you. She and I could have run off with or without the money. But I gave up my whole identity, my whole world to protect you."

"Funny, but it's hard to see it that way. In fact, it feels like I was the one who gave up *his* whole world to protect *you*, Dad. To protect your secret."

His old man shook his head slowly, then propped his elbows on the table to cradle his weathered face. For the second time in Barrett's life, he saw his father cry.

Chapter Sixteen

Nina knew that she needed to give Barrett his space. She'd driven by the Tenacity Inn two nights ago after leaving Uncle Stanley and Winona's, but she hadn't seen Barrett's truck there. Not that she would have stopped to tell him what Winona had said about Mayor Woodson being the wrong man.

On her way to work this morning, she again drove by the inn and didn't see his truck. Her stomach dropped. Ever since Barrett had returned to Tenacity, there'd been a warning in the back of her mind that he would eventually leave.

She just hadn't expected him to do it with another disappearing act instead of actually saying goodbye.

It took every ounce of self-control not to send him a message and ask him where he was. Nina had dropped quite a bomb on him when she'd told him about his father and June Woodson. It was reasonable that he might need some time to come to terms with the shocking revelation. If she pushed him away for good, then she would just have to live with the fact that things between the two of them were never meant to be.

But then this afternoon, she'd run into her future sister-in-law Ruby at the drugstore, and Julian's fiancée asked if Barrett was going to be back in town for Sunday dinner with the Sanchezes. When Nina didn't have an answer, Ruby said, "Well, let me know if he needs to book a room at the inn again and I'll see if Carol will let me give him the friends-and-family rate."

That was how Nina had found out that he'd officially checked out of the inn and left Tenacity. Possibly for good.

Not wanting to be alone but not wanting to go home where her parents were likely to ask her if she'd heard from Barrett, she thought for a second about heading to the Grizzly Bar to drown her potential heartbreak. But that was the place where she'd finally figured out the truth about the Woodson family's connection to the Deroy family.

Sure, the realization might have made her feel slightly vindicated, but at what cost? Had solving an old mystery been worth it if finding out the truth meant she would never see Barrett again?

It wasn't until she was driving by the Tenacity Social Club that she decided to pull over and stop. Some of her best memories with Barrett had been down those basement steps and inside that door. It might not have been the place to get her mind off of him, but at least it would feel familiar.

"You look like you could use a milkshake," Mike Cooper said when Nina sat down at the bar.

"You can say that again. Except instead of putting ice cream in the blender, could you use tequila instead?"

Mike set down a napkin as a coaster. "One margarita coming up."

When the bartender turned to make her drink, Nina looked down at the bar top and nearly groaned. Of course she would have chosen the one spot in the place that would make her think of Barrett all the more. She ran her fingers over the initials Barrett had once carved into the wood: *B and N 4ever.*

The back of her neck grew warm and tingly, the way it always did when she felt his presence. Except he wasn't here now. The only thing that remained of their love were their initials and a silly teenage promise. She muttered to herself, "More like 'B and N for a few days.'"

"Really?" Barrett's voice made her blink in surprise. "Because I was actually hoping for forever."

"You're back," she said just as Mike set a frosty drink in front of her.

"Are you talking to me or the margarita?" Barrett asked, then nodded at Mike, who'd pointed to the tap for the same beer he'd ordered last time they were here.

Nina's muscles sagged in relief at the knowledge that Barrett hadn't left for good. Yet they still retained a hint of tension because the last time she'd seen him, he'd been pretty upset at her. "I'm talking to whoever will make me feel like I'm not wasting my time."

"That's fair." He took the stool beside her. "I did run out on you a couple of days ago with no explanation. Then things kind of blew up in Whitehorn, and I thought it was only right to get my life settled over there before coming back here for you."

"You came back for me?" She took a sip of her drink, trying to act as nonchalant as possible. She knew better than to get her hopes up again. "Or you came back to finish clearing your name?"

"For you." He smiled, and her heart forced every doubt out of her body. "That is, if you're still willing to be seen in town with a Deroy after everything comes out."

She spun toward him so quickly her knees knocked into his. "Did Uncle Stanley tell you about Winona and her prediction that everyone had the wrong man? It wasn't Mayor Woodson who stole the money."

"I know," Barrett said, then thanked Mike for his beer. "It was his wife."

Nina nearly fell off her barstool. "You're telling me it was a scorned-mistress sort of thing? Mrs. Woodson was the one trying to frame you?"

Barrett shook his head. "No, and my dad has asked me not to refer to the love of his life as his quote mistress un-quote."

"That sounds like it was more than just an affair."

Barrett proceeded to tell her about a childhood love that would have sounded familiar to their own had they married other people. "As much as I want to be mad at my father for cheating on my mom, I have to ask myself if I would have done things differently in that situation. If I had returned to Tenacity to find you married, Nina, I would like to think that I would have done the right thing and given you up."

"Of course you would have, Barrett." She put a reassuring hand on his arm. "It would have been hard for both of us, but I'm sure we would have..."

Nina's voice faded as she realized how judgmental she must've sounded. She lowered her head, staring at the way her boots were now resting on the lower rung of his barstool, right between his. They'd always fit together like this, physically and emotionally gravitating toward one another like a magnetic connection that couldn't be pulled apart. The fifteen years they'd spent apart had felt like the longest years of her life. Yet once she saw Barrett again, it was almost as though no time had passed at all. Who was she to say that his dad and June Woodson weren't the same way? Who was she to say that her and Barrett's love was purer than theirs?

He lifted her chin, and the warmth in his brown eyes made her want to melt against him. "Luckily, we won't ever have to wonder how things would be between us if we weren't free to be together."

"Are you saying that we're free to be together now, Barrett?"

His hand moved to stroke her hair. "I'm free when it comes to you. But there is still so much damage that needs to be repaired, so many lies that need to be untangled. It's going to be messy, and people are still going to gossip about my family. I won't ever be able to get past the fact that an entire community—homeowners and businesspeople—suffered because of the choices my father made."

"It wasn't just your father, though. The Woodsons should be held accountable, too."

"I can't control any of that, Nina. And I no longer want to."

She nodded, ready to take a leap of faith with him. "So then we go back to Whitehorn. Nobody will blame you for not wanting to stay in Tenacity."

"You'd leave your hometown, your job, and your family to come with me?"

This time her nod was even more emphatic, and she moved her hands to his shoulders. "Of course I would. I didn't have that option when I was fourteen, but the only thing I've ever wanted was to be with you. You *are* my home, Barrett Déroy. I couldn't imagine living anywhere without you."

His arms went around her waist, and he pulled her—and her barstool—closer. "I love you so damn much, Nina Sanchez. For the past fifteen years, everything else in my life has felt like a lie. But you have always been the thing that is real. Our love is real."

She stood up, despite the fact that her legs had become wobbly at finally hearing him say the words she'd been hoping to hear for the past decade and a half. "Then what are you waiting for? I'm ready to leave the past in the past. Let's go put Big Betty in the trailer and drive her back home to the Double N."

Barrett squeezed her tighter, then shook his head. "No, I'm done with running and hiding. I need to make things right. I want to do something to help the town."

"How?"

"I'm not the wealthiest man in Montana, but I have done pretty well for myself as B.D. Jones. I'm thinking maybe I should start some sort of foundation to repair what's been broken. It's time I reinvest in Tenacity."

"Here?" Nina swallowed, trying not to become too giddy at the realization that she could finally have everything she ever wanted.

"Well, I heard that Tenacity High School hasn't hired a new football coach yet." Barrett smiled. "Plus, there's a decent-sized parcel of land off Juniper Road that I think Big Betty might like."

Nope, there was no way she could hold back this bubbling feeling of happiness inside of her. She easily returned his smile. "What about your horses? You told me they were Whitehorn horses."

"Luckily, I know a good horse trainer who can help them acclimate to their new home. Besides, my dad is currently staying at my ranch, which is why it took me so long to get back here to you. He and my mom have finally admitted that there's been too much strain on their marriage and that it would be best to go their separate ways. I helped my mom pack up what she wanted from their apartment, and she left this morning to drive to this artists' colony she heard about in New Mexico."

"I didn't know your mom was an artist," Nina said, as if this was the most shocking thing he'd said today.

"I don't think she is. But I guess she's been listening to a lot of self-realization podcasts lately, and I'm all for her exploring her independence and finding joy in something that makes her happy."

The door to the Social Club opened, and Brent Woodson walked in. She felt Barrett tense slightly, then relax when his formal rival gave them both a slight nod of acknowledgment and headed over to the other end of the bar.

Nina lowered her voice. "So what's going to happen between your father and you-know-who's mom?"

"That is not my concern," Barrett said. "Manny has already been over to give my old man a pep talk about how the first divorce is always the hardest and how he needs to learn how to be single for a while. I gave him Marshall's number and told him that he and June can figure out how to handle the case from here. I only care about one childhood sweetheart, and that's you. If you're still willing to have me."

She took a step closer, standing between his legs. "I have loved you since I was a little girl, Barrett Deroy. I've never stopped loving you."

"Good. Then marry me."

Nina laughed at his direct statement. "Are you asking me, or are you telling me?"

"You're not the only one in this relationship who doesn't like taking no for an answer." Barrett kissed her lightly on the lips.

"In that case, you better get used to hearing the word *yes*," she said, then kissed him deeply.

Epilogue

The Tenacity Midsummer Night's Bonfire was Nina's second-most favorite thing about living in Tenacity. The park still wasn't back to its glory days of fifteen years ago, but the green grass was heathier than ever, and most of the townspeople were fine lounging on their own blankets to hear a free concert, roast marshmallows, and enjoy the crisp night air.

The Stroms had donated some pallets from their feed store for the bonfire (after removing all the nails, of course), and the Hastingses had provided hay bales to use as benches for people like Uncle Stanley and Winona who required more seating options than just the ground.

Another dog owner was talking to Miles Parker and Renee Trent about how much better behaved Jasper and Bella were doing on their leashes compared to her young pup. Mike Cooper and Daniel Taylor were laughing at a funny story Jenna and Diego were telling them about trying to get a photo of Robbie with Big Betty and Noodles the goat.

The Coreys had set up a s'mores-making station for the kids, and Lucy Bernard and Noah Trent were helping his two-year-old triplets assemble gooey marshmallows between stacks of graham crackers and chocolate squares.

Josh Aventura was sitting with Amy Hawkins and several members of the Hawkins family, while Carol from Tenacity Inn was directing Grayson and a few members of the football team to take their water-balloon war with the cheerleaders over to the other side of the park.

Her parents had walked Emery and baby Jay over to the food stand the Castillos had set up, and Barrett had been relieved to see that they were only selling *buñuelos* tonight and not enchiladas suizas.

Julian and Ruby would be getting married in a few days, and soon after, Nina and Barrett would begin planning their own wedding. But for tonight, Nina just wanted to enjoy being in the town that she loved with the people she loved.

Nearly everyone had come out to the park tonight, including newcomer Marshall Gordon, who had gotten the middle finger from Mrs. Ferguson when he'd unknowingly parked his car in the spot she thought was reserved solely for her.

The only people notably absent were the Woodsons and Cecil Brewster, who was driving the Tenacity Shuttler route tonight and was supposed to pick up Mrs. Wheaton.

"The bonfire looks like it needs more wood," Barrett said, then gave Nina a kiss before jogging over to his truck where he'd loaded some of the logs he'd brought back from Whitehorn after the contractors removed the oak tree that had caused havoc with his water pipes.

Barrett Senior was still staying at the Double N, but Nina and Barrett had just closed escrow on the new ranch they'd bought together in Tenacity. They hadn't decided on a name for the property yet, but Barrett had already carved a wooden sign for the entrance that resembled what he'd written in the bar at the Tenacity Social Club all those years ago: B and N 4ever.

Luca dropped down to take a seat on Nina's blanket just as Brent Woodson approached the tailgate of Barrett's truck. She couldn't hear what the two rivals were saying, but Luca—who usually tried to play mediator between them—was keeping his distance for a reason, so maybe she should, too.

She nudged her brother, and under her breath she asked, "What do you think they're talking about?"

"It could be about the temporary defensive-coordinator position for the football team," Luca offered. Then he smirked slowly. "Or they could be talking about the fact that they were almost step-brothers once."

Nina playfully shoved her brother's arm. "Don't ever let Barrett hear you say that. We went out to Whitehorn last week to pick up the rest of his horses, and he couldn't stop cringing every time his dad referred to Mrs. Woodson as Junie."

Luca practically snorted.

"I know." Nina covered her mouth to keep from giggling. "Part of me wants to be scandalized by the affair and part of me wants to be angry at Mr. Deroy for keeping Barrett away all this time. But there's a teeny tiny romantic part of me that wants to see another pair of high school sweethearts finally get their shot at love."

"What about the part of you that wants to see the former mayor get payback for making everyone think it was Barrett who stole the money in the first place?"

Nina almost said something about karma but then caught sight of Barrett and Brent walking their way carrying the last load of firewood. The men dropped the logs near the fire, and for a second, she thought the light from the flames was playing tricks on her eyesight. She whispered to her brother, "Did they just shake hands?"

"That's what it looked like to me. At this rate, Barrett might ask Brent to be the best man at your wedding."

Barrett walked up just in time to hear Luca's prediction. "Not gonna happen, Luca. I picked you to be my best man way back when we were still in high school. So get that tux ready."

Luca made a groaning sound, but Nina could tell that her brother was secretly pleased. His best friend was officially back.

Barrett raised his mug of hot cocoa and said, "To a new day in Tenacity!"

Everyone around them cheered.

Soon, the real work would begin.

* * * * *

Don't miss the first installment of the new continuity
Montana Mavericks: Behind Closed Doors

The Maverick's Dating Deal
by New York Times *bestselling author Christine Rimmer*

On sale August 2025, wherever Harlequin books
and ebooks are sold.

And catch up with the books in the previous series,
Montana Mavericks: The Tenacity Social Club

The Maverick's Promise
by Melissa Senate

A Maverick's Road Home
by USA TODAY *bestselling author Catherine Mann*

All In with the Maverick
by Elizabeth Hrib

A Maverick Worth Waiting For
by USA TODAY *bestselling author Laurel Greer*

Maverick's Full House
by USA TODAY *bestselling author Tara Taylor Quinn*

Available now!

Harlequin Reader Service

Enjoyed your book?

Try the perfect subscription for Romance readers and get more great books like this delivered right to your door.

See why over 10+ million readers have tried Harlequin Reader Service.

Start with a Free Welcome Collection with free books and a gift—valued over $20.

Choose any series in print or ebook. See website for details and order today:

TryReaderService.com/subscriptions